ONE NIGHT OF SURRENDER

DARCY BURKE

Surrender to love!

Darcy Burke

ISBN: 1944576487
ISBN-13: 9781944576486

Book design: © Darcy Burke.
Book Cover Design © The Midnight Muse Designs.
Cover image: © Period Images.
Editing: Linda Ingmanson.

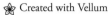 Created with Vellum

CHAPTER 1

*I*sabelle Cortland tripped as she stepped over the threshold into the Duke of East-leigh's town house. Not a slight stumble from which she recovered, but a full-out loss of balance that sent her sprawling onto the marble floor in an ungainly heap, her skirts riding up the back of her legs in a most humiliating manner.

Was it too much to hope he hadn't seen her? Or that she could melt into the gleaming white stone?

"Mrs. Cortland!" The voice of her employer, Lord Barkley, hit her just before he grasped her elbow. "Are you all right?"

"Fine, thank you." Placing her palms against the floor, she pushed herself up and brought her legs beneath her. Once she was on her knees, Lord Barkley helped her up.

Caroline, the younger of Isabelle's two charges, stepped forward and brushed at Isabelle's dress. "You're all disheveled now. Let me help." All of ten years old, Caroline was always quick to offer assistance as well as her opinion.

"Thank you." Isabelle looked around the hall in agitation. He wasn't here. Thank goodness.

"Are you certain you aren't injured?" Lord Barkley asked.

Just her pride, but even that had been spared in the absence of the duke. "I am certain."

"His Grace apologizes for not greeting you personally," the butler said. "He will be home shortly."

Lord Barkley straightened. "Quite all right. Deuced hospitable of him to allow us to stay."

Indeed it was. They'd arrived in London that morning only to find the town house Lord Barkley had leased for the Season was not yet habitable above the ground floor. It was undergoing refurbishment and would be ready in a fortnight—or so they'd been promised. In the meantime, Lord Barkley had asked his friend the Duke of Eastleigh if they could stay with him. The duke, who Lord Barkley assured her was a generous and magnanimous fellow, had invited them to stay as long as they needed.

The duke was also arrogant, clever, and far more charming than anyone had a right to be. At least he had been ten years ago. Was he still the same?

She doubted she would find out. Isabelle planned to keep as far out of his way as possible. If she were lucky, she would endure the entire stay without ever clapping eyes on him. Which meant she'd best flee upstairs with alacrity.

Turning to the butler, she offered him a smile. "May I accompany my charges to their chamber?" She glanced toward Caroline and her sister, Beatrice, who was older by three years. Their brother, Douglas, was at Oxford.

"Of course." The butler inclined his head toward a white-haired woman with a kind smile and bright, earnest eyes. "Mrs. Watkins will show you up."

The housekeeper, for that was what she had to

be, beamed at Isabelle and the girls. "Come along. I have the perfect chamber for you dears." She started toward the stairs.

Isabelle gestured for the girls to precede her.

"Barkley! Welcome to my humble home. I'm so pleased to see you."

Isabelle nearly tripped again as she placed her foot on the bottom step. The unmistakable—even after all this time—voice of the duke locked her breath in her lungs.

"Humble, ha!" Lord Barkley's deep chuckle echoed in the hall. "Thank you for inviting us to stay. The governess is just taking my girls upstairs."

Isabelle forced herself to move. If she hurried, she could hopefully avoid meeting the duke. Rather, re-meeting the duke. Oh, this was going to be a *disaster*.

"You can make the girls' acquaintance later," Lord Barkley said, and Isabelle finally breathed.

There was a pause, and during that pause, Isabelle felt certain the duke's eyes were boring into her back with all-seeing intensity. At any moment, he would call her by name and the secrets she'd long buried would be exposed. She'd lose her dignity, her post, and the goal that she was working so hard to achieve: her school.

"I'll look forward to meeting them." The duke's response made Isabelle's insides curl with envy. Envy? She didn't want to see him. She *shouldn't* want to see him.

She followed the housekeeper and her charges up, and when the staircase turned, she kept her face averted from the hall—right up until the last moment. Then she stole a glance at the man whose image was seared in her mind for all time.

He looked precisely the same, as far as she could tell at this distance. Tall, broad-shouldered, with those bow-shaped lips that had no business on a man's face.

They ascended past the first floor up to the second, and Mrs. Watkins led them to the right and then into a well-appointed bedchamber that overlooked the square below. "Here we are," Mrs. Watkins said. "Your things will be up shortly."

Caroline dashed to the window and looked down. "What a lovely square."

"Is this your first time in London?" Mrs. Watkins asked.

Caroline turned from the window. "Yes. We're going to visit the British Museum and Gunter's, and Beatrice is hoping to shop on Bond Street. Papa said we can't because Mama didn't come with us. She had to go take care of Great-Auntie again. She's sick."

Mrs. Watkins's brow creased, and she gave Caroline a heartfelt nod. "I'm sorry to hear that."

"I'll convince him to let Mrs. Cortland take us," Beatrice said firmly. "I already asked him, and he said he'd think about it."

Shopping on Bond Street? Isabelle wouldn't know the slightest thing. Traipsing around London with the girls sounded equal parts harrowing and exciting.

"You've been to London before, then?" Mrs. Watkins asked Isabelle.

She shook her head. "No."

"Well then, this shall be an adventure for all of you!" The footman arrived with the girls' luggage, and Mrs. Watkins directed him to place it over by the armoire.

"Where will Mrs. Cortland sleep?" Caroline asked. "At home, her room is just up the stairs from ours."

"Her room is upstairs here too." Mrs. Watkins tipped her head toward Isabelle. "Shall I show you?"

Isabelle smiled in appreciation. "Thank you, but I'll stay and help the girls unpack. I'm sure I can find my way if you give me the direction."

"Just up the stairs—the door is at the end of the gallery—then to the right, second door on your left. I could send a maid up to unpack their things," the housekeeper offered.

"Thank you, but that isn't necessary." Isabelle was more than happy to help the girls herself. She loved them as much as if they were her own children, in part because she didn't have any and never would.

The housekeeper nodded. "I'll leave you to it, then." She departed with a smile, closing the door softly behind her.

"When will we meet the duke?" Caroline asked as Isabelle opened and began to unpack their valises. "I've never met a duke before."

Isabelle hid a smile because Caroline had made that statement no less than half a dozen times since they'd learned they would be staying with the Duke of Eastleigh.

The name alone had caused Isabelle a fright. She'd never thought to hear it again, let alone be staying in his house. When she'd taken this governess position in Staffordshire five years ago, she never dreamed she'd come face-to-face with Valentine Fairfax, the Duke of Eastleigh again.

And hopefully she wouldn't.

Could she really stay here for a fortnight without seeing him? She was going to do her best.

"Maybe we'll meet the duke at dinner," Beatrice said, answering Caroline's question about meeting the duke. "If we're invited."

Isabelle suffered another moment's panic. What if Val invited them to dinner, and what if, God forbid, that invitation included her? She'd occasionally dined with Lord and Lady Barkley and the children, but hopefully, a duke's household was far more formal, and she and the children would be excluded. "I'm not sure you should expect to dine at the duke's table," Isabelle said as she handed a stack of undergarments to Beatrice to put away in the dresser.

"I suppose not," Beatrice said, opening a drawer. "But it would be wonderful, wouldn't it?"

Caroline snorted. "You would think so."

Beatrice's dark curls bounced against her narrow shoulders as she pursed her lips and threw her sister an irritated stare. "Who's to say I'll ever have cause to dine with a duke again?"

Indeed. Isabelle never had and hoped she never would. Not this duke and not any duke. She was not and had never been like Beatrice, who looked forward to her come out and being the belle of the Season. Isabelle just wanted to educate girls like Beatrice and help them understand there was more to life than dukes and balls. While Beatrice had soaked up knowledge like a dry biscuit dipped in tea, she remained steadfastly enchanted with becoming a debutante and shopping the Marriage Mart—for now. The girl was, after all, only thirteen.

Caroline held her arms out for a stack of clothing to put away. "Do you suppose he has a library?"

"Probably." Isabelle had no idea if London homes had the same sorts of libraries as country houses, but the Val she remembered had been an avid reader, so she suspected he would. Unless he wasn't the Val she remembered. Ten years was an awfully long time, and they had been incredibly young…

And naïve.

"I hope so," Caroline said. "Perhaps we should go look after we unpack?"

Isabelle gave her a warm but firm look. "I think it's best if you both rest for a bit while I go upstairs and see to my things."

Caroline exhaled with disappointment. The girl hated to sit still. "If you say so."

They finished unpacking, and Isabelle gave them both instructions to read and practice writing their Latin. She'd return in an hour for their lesson.

"Is there no schoolroom?" Beatrice asked.

"I don't know." Mrs. Watkins hadn't mentioned it, and Isabelle wasn't sure she wanted to ask. To do so might draw attention to herself, and she planned to be as invisible as possible.

"I hope so, because this room only has that small desk and a single chair." Beatrice was, unfortunately, correct.

Isabelle supposed she would have to ask, but she'd bring it up with Lord Barkley and leave it to him to sort things out. "I'll speak to your father. Time to read." When they were ensconced on the bed with their books, Isabelle left.

Closing the door behind her, she recalled what the housekeeper had said. *The door is at the end of the gallery—to the right, second door on your left.* Or had she said to the left, second door on your right? Exhaling, Isabelle strode to the end of the gallery. She put her hand on the latch and paused. Had Mrs. Watkins meant this end of the gallery?

Isabelle looked back the way she'd come. Suddenly, the door in front of her opened, and standing there in all his ducal glory, his sun-gold hair swept back from the wide plane of his forehead and his jade-green eyes widening in surprise, was the man she'd tried—and failed—to forget.

~

*V*al stared at the woman standing outside his door as if she were an apparition. Was she? She had to be. Why else would she be there?

He blinked, closing his eyes with purpose and keeping them shut for a moment. But when he opened them again, she was still there.

"Isabelle?" She was older, of course, and far more beautiful than he remembered. He hadn't dreamed that could be possible. Most of her light brown hair was pulled back in a rather severe chignon, but two curls bobbed in front of each ear. A faint pink blush stained her angled cheekbones, and her full coral lips were parted in surprise.

Now she blinked, her dark lashes briefly closing over her vivid cobalt eyes. Finally, she said, "Yes."

"I can't believe it." He reached for her, but she took a step back. He frowned. "What are you doing here?"

"I am governess to the Misses Spelman."

"Governess? How on earth did you become a governess? I thought you were supposed to marry… some gentleman." Val couldn't begin to recall the man's name. If she hadn't married him—damn, was that his fault? Val's insides swirled with discomfort.

"I did."

Relief poured through him.

"He passed away six years ago." Her placid features didn't reveal a hint of emotion beyond solemnity.

"I'm so sorry. I did hear that your father died, and I was very sorry to hear it. He was a wonderful man, an exemplary teacher." He'd been warden of Merton College, and several of Val's friends had been matriculated there. "Wasn't it around that time?"

"It was," she said quietly. "I lost my father in January and my husband just three months later."

His heart ached for her that she'd lost so much in such a short span. "That must not have been easy."

"No." She clasped her hands before her and

wrung them together briefly as she looked to the side. "I'd hoped to avoid seeing you, Your Grace. I was looking for the stairs. To my room on the third floor."

"They are at the other end of the gallery," he said rather absentmindedly as he focused on the other things she'd said. "Why would you want to avoid me? And don't call me 'Your Grace.'"

She arched a brow, and oh, how he remembered that expression. She had a way of looking at him that was equal parts seductive and haughty. It had never failed to arouse him, and he'd be damned if she wasn't doing it again. Suddenly, he was eighteen years old—as he was when he'd first met her—and absolutely smitten.

"What *should* I call you?" she asked.

"What you always called me."

She clamped her lips together and looked instantly more like a governess than the woman who'd captivated him as a lad. "I can't do that. You're a duke, and I'm a governess. We shouldn't even be standing here talking." She abruptly turned and started along the gallery.

Val stepped out of his private sitting room and leapt after her. He reached for her elbow, and the moment his hand closed around her sleeve, he felt a swooning sensation in the pit of his belly.

She pulled her arm from his grip with a gasp. Turning toward him, her eyes blazing a cold fire, she opened her mouth, and he actually leaned toward her, craving her indignation. She'd delivered him so many set downs when he'd begun to flirt with her. It had taken months for her to finally admit she was attracted to him too.

But he never got to hear what she was about to say, because they'd stopped in front of Barkley's room, and the door opened to reveal the baron.

Barkley looked from Val to Isabelle and back to Val again. "I see you've met our governess."

"Yes—"

Anything Val might have said next was drowned out by her response. "Yes, we've just met. I'm afraid I got turned around looking for the stairs. His Grace was kind enough to direct me. If you'll just excuse me."

Val looked toward her, narrowing his eyes slightly. They'd just met?

Her gaze met his, and in the depths of her eyes, he saw a silent plea. Apparently, she didn't want him to say they knew each other. What did she think he would do, reveal the *extent* to which they knew each other?

"Before you rush off, Mrs. ..."

"Cortland," she supplied.

Not knowing her name certainly supported her insistence that they'd just met. To him, she'd been Isabelle Highmore, the most beautiful girl he'd ever seen.

"Before you rush off, Mrs. Cortland, I do hope you'll join us for dinner."

Isabelle looked toward Barkley, who inclined his head, then returned her attention to Val. "What time shall I have the girls ready?"

The girls? Barkley's daughters. Val hadn't invited *them*. But to exclude them now, in front of their father no less, would be rude. The fact was that he didn't even want Barkley at the bloody dinner. He wanted Isabelle alone so he could learn every single thing she'd done in the past decade.

"Seven," Val said.

Isabelle dipped a curtsey and turned. Val tried very hard not to stare at her swaying backside as she walked to the other end of the gallery. With great reluctance, he turned to Barkley. "How long has Mrs. Cortland been in your employ?"

Barkley cocked his head to the side and stuck his lower lip out while he pondered the question. "Going on five years now, I think. Yes, has to be five. When Caroline had her fifth birthday, we hired Mrs. Cortland to tutor the girls. When she wrote and said who her father had been, I knew she was perfect for the job. Truth be told, she's more clever than I imagined a woman could be."

Val stared at the man, momentarily bereft of speech at his implication. Rather than call out Barkley's rudeness—and idiocy—Val ignored the asinine comment. Unlike Barkley, Val wasn't the least surprised by Isabelle's intellect. She'd always had her nose in a book. It was one of the things he'd liked best about her. In fact, the times they'd sat together on a bench outside simply reading side by side were some of his favorite memories. "It sounds as though you are quite fortunate to have Mrs. Cortland."

"Indeed we are," Barkley said with a nod. "Are we still having that glass of brandy before dinner?"

Val wanted to interrogate Barkley about Isabelle —did she still love Voltaire, and did she still snort if she laughed too hard? Instead, he pasted on a smile and clapped the baron on his shoulder. "Yes, let's."

They went downstairs, and all Val could think of was the woman upstairs and how in the hell he was going to get her alone.

CHAPTER 2

*H*e couldn't mean for her to sit next to him.

Isabelle stared at the chair to the right of the head of the table, where Val—she couldn't help but think of him by what she'd called him ten years ago no matter how hard she tried— would undoubtedly sit.

"Sorry to be running late," Val said as he strode into the dining room, causing them all to turn. "I had an urgent matter." Smiling, he went to his chair and looked around at them—Lord Barkley to his left, Beatrice to her father's left, Caroline across from Beatrice, and Isabelle next to her. As well as next to Val.

"Shall we sit?" their host suggested, and Isabelle had her answer. Yes, he absolutely meant for her to sit beside him.

Logically, it made sense for the two adults to sit closest to the head of the table. That didn't stop Isabelle from wondering if he had a motive. Was that because she wanted him to have one?

Mentally chiding herself, she took her seat and resisted the urge to drink her entire glass of wine to calm her nerves. Instead, she didn't even take a sip, reasoning that she needed to keep every wit about her.

"I hope you're all settled in," Val said. "And that you'll let Sadler know if there is anything you require."

"It's just splendid, Your Grace," Lord Barkley said jovially as the first course was served. "Capital of you to open your bachelor home to our family." He chuckled good-naturedly.

Isabelle waited for her employer to ask about the need for a schoolroom. She'd brought it up when they'd arrived in the dining room. When he said nothing, she contemplated how she might broach the subject. However, before she could do so, Caroline beat them all to it.

The youngest person at the table addressed their host without blinking. "Actually, Your Grace, we do need something."

Her father shot her a look of pure horror. "Caroline, you will not speak unless His Grace addresses you."

"It's quite all right," Val said, looking toward Caroline with a warm smile. "What do you need?"

"A schoolroom." She glanced at Isabelle. "Mrs. Cortland suggested we might use your library."

"Did she?" Val murmured.

Though Isabelle didn't look at him—she was trying so hard not to—she felt his gaze sweeping over her like a warm summer breeze, welcome and invigorating.

"*If* you have a library," Beatrice put in.

"I most certainly have a library, and it is at your disposal."

Lord Barkley frowned at his daughters. "We don't wish to put you out." He turned a flattering smile toward Val. "I'd planned to ask you about a space for them to learn. Later."

"There is no inconvenience." He looked directly at Isabelle, and she couldn't ignore him. Nor could she afford to lose herself in the depths of his still-seductive gaze. "Tell me when you need the library, and it's yours."

She could almost imagine he'd said, *Tell me when you need me, and I'm yours*. But he hadn't, of course, and she silently cursed her fanciful, traitorous mind.

Isabelle averted her eyes. It was so hard to look at him and not feel a jolt of awareness. Or worse, longing. "We conduct lessons in the morning and again in the afternoon, though I anticipate spending some afternoons on excursions while we're in London."

"The library shall be yours every morning and in the afternoons. I will make sure you are as undisturbed as possible."

"Thank you." Isabelle met his eyes again and was instantly taken back to a decade ago, to a time when someone had looked at her like that, as if he wanted to know her—as if he *did* know her. Aside from a close connection to Beatrice and Caroline as their governess, she'd been utterly alone these past six years, and to feel this sense of...belonging was almost overwhelming.

She spent the rest of the dinner struggling to appear serene and unaffected whilst the memory of her time with Val and his current proximity made her heart pound and her insides flutter. She feared Lord Barkley would detect the familiarity between them and demand to know what was going on. Would it be terrible to admit they'd known each other—platonically, of course—once? Perhaps not, but it was a risk she dare not take.

When dinner was over, Isabelle was relieved to remove the girls from the dining room with the utmost haste. After seeing them to bed, she'd hurried to her third-floor retreat, where she prepared for bed and immediately buried her nose in a book that couldn't hope to hold her attention.

After an hour, she was about to give up when a light knock drew her to turn her head toward the door. Her first thought was that it could be Val. Just as quickly, she told herself that was silly. He wouldn't be so foolish as to visit her up here. She was simply allowing him too much space in her head. No more.

It was likely Caroline, who sometimes grew scared in the night and would come to Isabelle's room. It happened less now than it had in years past, but they were in a strange house.

Isabelle set her book on the tiny nightstand and slipped from her narrow bed. The room was smaller than what she was used to, but it had a window with a charming view of the garden below.

She opened the door and sucked in a breath. "Val."

Garbed in the immaculately tailored suit of clothing he'd worn to dinner, he grinned, and her entire body heated in response. "You *do* remember my name."

"You shouldn't be here." That was all she managed to get out before he pushed past her and strode into the room.

He frowned as he surveyed the chamber. "This is very small."

"You act as though you've never been up here."

"Not never, but not in some time." He straightened and gave her a decisive nod. "I'll move you downstairs."

Closer to him. That was a terrible notion. "No, you won't."

He took a step toward her, the frown returning. "A governess isn't a servant."

"Nor is she a member of the family." Footsteps

on the stairs filled her with alarm. "You need to go. You can't be in here."

He rotated his head, presenting his ear toward the door and took another step forward. "Is someone coming?"

"Yes," she hissed.

"Then I can't very well leave. I'd walk right by whoever it is." He sounded utterly unconcerned.

Isabelle closed the door with a firm click. Then she spun around to glare at him. "Are you trying to get me tossed out?"

"I would never toss you out. And no, I'm not trying to have your employment terminated. Though I will say I never imagined I'd see you as a governess." His gaze dipped over her as if he were assessing what he *had* seen her as—and she didn't want to know.

Too aware of his lingering attention and the fact that she wore only a night rail covered with a rather thin dressing gown, she crossed her arms across her chest and gave him a cool stare. "You need to go."

"And I shall. Soon. After we...talk." He looked around the room once more, and his gaze settled on the diminutive chair situated in the corner next to her miniscule nightstand.

"We have nothing to talk about," Isabelle said.

He moved to the chair and sat down. "Come now, after a decade, there is plenty to discuss. I could sit here with you all night."

All night. They'd done that once. But they hadn't been sitting. Or talking. Well, there had been *some* talking. And *some* sitting...of sorts. She blushed at the memory.

He gave her a sly look. "What are you thinking about?"

She shook her head, pushing the recollection away. "Nothing. Really, you need to go. I can't allow you to jeopardize my position."

"We could just have told Barkley that we're old friends."

Isabelle squeezed her fingertips into her biceps. "We aren't."

"Yes, we are. We wouldn't have to tell him the part about being lovers." He said it so casually, so offhandedly, as if it were absolutely ordinary. How could it be when it had been the most extraordinary experience of her life? When she measured her days in terms of before Val and after Val? "Why did you lie to him and say we'd just met?" His query fished her back from the abyss of the past.

"It seemed easier." And safer. They'd had to hide even their friendship at Oxford. The students were not allowed to fraternize with women, particularly the daughters of wardens who were, in turn, not supposed to fraternize with the students. They'd stolen time together here and there, mostly just to talk and read and talk about what they'd read.

He was staring at her as if he expected her to say more. As if he expected her to say she'd been wrong and of course they could reveal their friendship.

"You really need to go," she repeated.

Naturally, he didn't move. He'd always been stubborn, especially in their debates. His gaze strayed to her nightstand, and he picked up the battered book she'd set atop it. "Still reading French literature, I see. Oh, and it's one of our favorites." He gave her a dazzling smile.

"It was one of my favorites before it was one of yours."

"True. I keep a copy in my bedchamber." His gaze met hers, and the intensity of his stare made her knees weak.

"Why?" Where had that word come from? She hadn't thought it, but her lips had whispered it.

"Because it reminds me of you." He set down her worn copy of *Les Liaisons dangereuses*.

"Val, you really have to go." She sounded like a parrot that only knew how to say one thing.

He rose from the chair and came around the bed. "If you insist, but first tell me why you're a governess. What happened to your husband?"

"I told you, he died."

"Didn't he leave you any money?"

"What he left me with was debt, which my inheritance from my father settled. Thankfully, I am able to provide for myself. I'm quite happy in my current position." While that was true, it wasn't what she'd ever expected. She'd expected her own household, a husband, children.

"You had no children with him?" Val asked, seeming to have followed the course of her thoughts.

"You are too familiar," she said, growing uncomfortable with the direction of their conversation—because she could find comfort in it. When was the last time someone had spoken to her, really spoken *to* her?

"I should hope so," he said softly. "I know you rather well." He'd moved to stand just in front of her, so close that she could easily put her hands on him.

"You *knew* me. That was a long time ago." And yet his scent of pine and sandalwood was as familiar as the book on her nightstand.

"Can you be that different?" He studied her, his eyes caressing her as if he touched her.

She suddenly longed for that touch, as she had on so many occasions in the last decade, particularly in the early years. Over time, she'd learned to store her memories of him in the back of her mind, only bringing them forth when she allowed herself to feel vulnerable.

"Yes. As you must be." Like her, he'd been wed.

The marriage had to have affected him, as hers had impacted her. "I was sorry to read in the newspaper that your wife had died."

His jaw tightened, but only for a moment, and she wondered if she'd imagined the reaction. "We have both been unlucky in marriage, it seems."

There was a moment of silence between them. Marriage was something they had never discussed. She'd never dreamed a duke could marry someone like her, and he'd certainly never offered. They'd stolen their one night together and knew it would have to last them forever.

She still couldn't quite grasp that he was standing in front of her. That she could reach out and touch him. Or that there was a bed right behind him.

"You have to *go*." She turned toward the door.

He moved to stand in front of it, putting his back against the wood. "And I *will*. This is just so… strange. And wonderful. Don't you think so?" When she didn't respond, he continued, "I never thought to see you again, and yet here you are. It feels like a gift."

She blinked and tipped her head to the side, wondering what he meant exactly and not daring to presume. "Of what?"

He glanced up toward the low ceiling. "I don't know… It's just unexpected."

It was past time to put an end to whatever he was trying to do. "I will only be here a fortnight. I will try to stay out of your way, and I expect you to do the same, just as I expect you to keep our past… secret. I can't afford to lose this position." Besides, she loved Beatrice and Caroline, and she would be devastated to leave them before they no longer needed her. Even then, it would be difficult.

"If you lose your position—which you won't— I'll take care of you."

The air escaped her lungs in a whoosh, and she gaped at him, her arms dropping to her sides. "You aren't propositioning—"

His eyes widened. "No, *no*. I wasn't. I only meant that you needn't ever worry about your future. I would ensure you are safe."

"You can't do that. That would be...scandalous!" Her father would spin in his grave.

"No one would need to know."

She shook her head. "Absolutely not. I'm not a woman of loose morals." But she *had* been. Once. With him. "What happened between us was a mistake." She looked away because she couldn't bear to look at him as she told the lie she'd forced herself to believe.

"Don't say that." His voice was low and dark and raw.

"It's the truth. Now, go. Please." She looked at him then, her gaze pleading. "Your Grace."

He pressed his lips together, his mouth tensing. Then he did the unthinkable. He lifted his hand and stroked her cheek. Her body wanted to lean forward and fall against him, to welcome his touch, to seek it. Steeling herself, she stood ramrod still as her insides threatened to loosen and fall apart.

"I still care for you, and I *would* help you. All you need do is ask." He dropped his hand, then turned and left.

As soon as the door was closed, she placed her palm against the wood. The heat of him was still there from where he'd pressed up against it. He would help her if she'd just ask... He could probably make her dream of starting a school for girls come true, but she wouldn't ask. She *couldn't*.

Closing her eyes, she put her hand on the door as if it were him and allowed all the feelings and memories she worked so hard to suppress. His hand with hers. His lips on hers. His body in hers.

A wild craving she hadn't felt in some time washed over her. It was going to be a very long fortnight.

CHAPTER 3

The following evening, Val walked into the Wicked Duke, the tavern he owned with his good friend, the Duke of Colehaven, in the Haymarket. Heads turned and mugs clanked together with a rousing chorus of "Eastleigh!" Val performed a courtly bow, presenting his most elegant leg with a flourish.

Straightening, he made his way to the bar, which ran along the back wall of the primary salon. It was half ten, and the place was packed, so Val was stopped several times as he wove through the tables. When he arrived at the bar, Doyle already had his tankard—stamped with Eastleigh—filled with ale.

Val picked up the mug. "Is this Cole's latest?"

"It is. He said you were keen to try it." Doyle, the tavern's manager, waited expectantly while Val sampled the ale.

Rich and slightly bitter, the brew was delicious. "He's crafted another fine beer, not that I had any doubt."

"Where's Barkley tonight?" Doyle asked, likely because they'd arrived together the night before, and Val had told him Barkley was staying with him.

"He had other engagements this evening, but he'll be in, I'm sure."

"Once you come to the Wicked Duke, you don't want to go anywhere else." Doyle looked toward the nearest table. "Am I right, lads?"

They all lifted their mugs, and Doyle chuckled, the flesh around his light blue eyes crinkling with humor.

"How is it having Barkley and his family stay with you?" Doyle asked. "He's got children, hasn't he?"

Val nodded. "I only saw them for dinner last night." Which meant he hadn't seen their governess today either. He'd been tempted to duck into the library under the pretense of finding a book, but had decided not to bother them. Isabelle had seemed genuinely concerned that she could lose her position if their past connection was known.

And what connection was that? They hadn't seen each other in a decade. They were nothing more than acquaintances anymore. The realization stung, and yet what else should he have expected?

"Saw who?" The Duke of Colehaven arrived at the bar, and Doyle handed him his own mug emblazoned with "Colehaven."

"My houseguests," Val said.

"Has Barkley's family turned your household upside down?" Cole asked.

"No." But their governess was turning him inside out. "As I was just telling Doyle, I rarely see them. Anyway, it's only for a fortnight. Maybe less."

"You're a good friend." Cole drank the ale and looked appreciatively at the tankard. "This is fantastic beer, if I do say so myself."

"You're Barkley's friend too," Val pointed out. "Weren't you the one who introduced us? Barkley might have asked to stay with you if you weren't preparing to wed."

"He wouldn't want to come to my house. Diana has already launched her reorganization plan, and nothing is sacred." Cole shuddered for comedic effect, but Val saw the underlying tenderness in his friend's eyes. He was well and truly smitten. Had Val looked like that before he'd wed Louisa? Had he looked like that ten years ago when he'd known Isabelle?

He could ask Cole, who'd been present during both periods. But what did it matter? Louisa had been a licentious liar, and whatever he and Isabelle had shared had been fleeting—they'd known it then, and he knew it now. Even so, he couldn't resist telling Cole she was back.

Val picked up his tankard and looked to Cole. "Sit with me in the private salon for a bit."

Cole grabbed his ale and followed Val into the private salon, which was a smaller, quieter space with tables surrounded by plush, high-backed chairs perfectly situated for discreet conversations. They went to their favorite table set into the corner near the fireplace. No one sat there unless invited by one of them.

The private salon was fairly unpopulated this evening, with just a few tables sporting occupants. Which was good since Val was feeling particularly secretive.

Once they were seated with their backs to the walls, Cole sipped his ale before setting his mug on the polished table. "Is there anything amiss?"

"Amiss? No. Why would you think that?"

Cole shrugged. "You sounded serious when you asked to come in here."

"It isn't serious. It's—" Val ran his hand through his hair and felt a lock tumble over his forehead as it was wont to do. Someday, he'd learn to stop raking his fingers through the style his valet prided himself on perfecting, but today was not that day. "Hell, I don't know what it is." He locked eyes with Cole, who'd been his closest friend for nigh on fifteen years when they'd been green lads in their first year at Oxford. "Barkley brought his governess. It's Isabelle."

Cole stared at him, mirroring the disbelief Val had felt when he'd first seen her yesterday. Then he leaned forward and whispered, as if they weren't in a secluded location in a nearly empty room, "Isabelle Highmore?"

Val nodded as he settled back against the chair. He could've almost believed he'd dreamed her presence, but telling Cole somehow made it real. "Isabelle Cortland now. She's widowed, and her father died."

"I remember hearing he'd passed. She's Barkley's governess now?"

"For the past five years. It's bloody bizarre, Cole."

Cole blew out a breath. "I can imagine. Well, maybe I can't. It's been ten years since you've seen her. Did she remember you?"

Val stared at Cole as if he'd just spouted utter nonsense, which he had. "Of course she remembered me. She also wants nothing to do with me."

"How do you know—" Cole narrowed his hazel eyes. "Did you proposition her?"

"No! Christ, she thought I did too."

"If she thought so, you probably did."

"I only said I would help her if she needed it." Val exhaled with frustration. "I couldn't believe she'd become a governess. I never envisioned her in that role."

Cole snorted. "And because you never envisioned it, how could it be true?"

Val sat back with a scowl. "Perhaps I shouldn't have brought this up."

"My apologies. Why *did* you bring it up?"

"Because it's notable?" While Val had mostly put Isabelle from his mind after he'd wed Louisa, he still thought of her from time to time. Their one night together had been a singular occasion, a night he never thought to duplicate. "We shared something special."

"It was," Cole said slowly. "Is it still? Even after Louisa?"

Cole, of course, knew the damage Louisa had done. One could endure only so much from a profligate wife before one's general opinion of women and, more precisely, of marriage, plummeted.

"It will always be." Val realized he'd thought of Isabelle more after Louisa had died, perhaps not consciously, but he'd dreamed of her many times, of a life that maybe could have been.

"And now she's sleeping under your roof," Cole said. "How long will temptation be at your door?"

"A fortnight." No, less than that now. "Thirteen days. Or thereabouts."

"Are you hoping to repeat what you did at Oxford?" Cole leaned back against his chair with his tankard in his hand.

"We can't." But if Val were being honest with himself, yes, he hoped to.

"You don't sound terribly convinced."

No, he didn't, and suddenly Val knew why he'd wanted to talk to his friend. "I need you to convince me, dammit."

"You said she wanted nothing to do with you. That tells you everything you need to know. Keep your distance as you suffer through the next thirteen days and then carry on with your life." Cole drank from his mug and set it on the table.

"That's easy for you to say as you're about to marry the woman you love and who loves you in return."

Cole gaped at him in surprise. "Do you love Isabelle?"

"No." Val would never risk that again, not after Louisa. "I only meant that it's easy for you to dish out advice because you're so bloody happy."

"I'm not sure that makes any sense whatsoever, but if there's one thing I do recall, it's that when it comes to Isabelle Highmore—Cortland, whatever—you never made much sense."

That was probably true. He'd been consumed by her wit and intellect and enthralled with her beauty and charm.

"So I must stay away from her." It wasn't a question but a warning to himself. Cole was right.

Cole gave a single nod and an apologetic stare. "It sounds as if that's best. If she were interested in you, however, that might be a different story."

"You mean if she wanted to return to where we left off ten years ago?" Hell, what would he do then? Seduce her in the tiny bedroom nestled under the eaves of his town house? Invite her to share his bedchamber?

"It's a moot question." Cole looked down at his tankard. "Forget I said that."

Val was certain he wouldn't. Even if it was just a hazy notion in the back of his mind, he might forever dream about what he would do if Isabelle showed him the slightest inclination that she wanted him again. What would he do—take her as his mistress, or surrender to just one night as they'd done ten years ago?

"Unless you wanted to marry her," Cole said, snapping Val from his reverie.

"What?" Val narrowed his eyes briefly.

"You could marry her, if you wanted."

Val shook his head at Cole. "You seem to forget to whom you're speaking."

"You just told me that Isabelle was special."

"No, I said we *shared* something special."

Cole dropped his chin and regarded Val as if he were mad or an idiot or both. "You really want to debate semantics? I know better than anyone how Louisa tortured you, how deservedly bitter you are, but this is Isabelle. Surely she is different."

Surely. The only thing Val was sure of was that he wasn't going to open himself up to heartache again. Not to recapture a spectacular night. Not for anything.

"Once again spoken like a man whose happy future is secure." Val lifted his mug. "Let us drink to that."

"What are we toasting?" The voice belonged to Jack Barrett, who'd just arrived at their table.

"Cole's happiness," Val said. "Sit. We're drinking Cole's latest recipe."

Cole waved the barmaid over as Jack sat down at the table.

"I hope it's bitter as hell," Jack said wearily. "I need something to wash away the day I've had. It's a bloody tempest in the Commons since the attack on the Prince Regent." As the conversation turned to matters concerning the country, Cole slid Val a look that clearly communicated he'd be standing by should Val need him.

But Val wouldn't need him. He didn't need anyone.

CHAPTER 4

On the third day of their stay at Val's town house, Isabelle allowed herself to feel a modicum of relief. She'd steadfastly avoided their host and, because of her efforts, hadn't seen him since he'd barged into her room that first night.

Every morning, she dined in the breakfast room with the girls, where they also had luncheon, and in between, they conducted schoolwork in the library, which was every bit as spectacular as Isabelle had imagined. She'd stayed up far too late the past two nights reading *Waverley* and, as they finished breakfast, was eager to see what other delights she might find today.

"Shall we repair to the library?" Isabelle asked the girls.

Before they could respond, their father came into the breakfast room with a broad smile. "I hope you don't have anything planned for lessons this afternoon, Mrs. Cortland. The dowager duchess is coming to take the girls—and you—shopping."

Beatrice squealed with delight, while Caroline's reaction was far more reserved. "What about Gunter's?" Caroline asked.

"The trip will include a stop at Gunter's after

you've finished on Bond Street. I will meet you there, and I may even have a surprise." He winked at them, and the girls erupted into excited chatter.

Isabelle exhaled with resignation. Getting them to attend to their studies this morning was going to require a great deal of effort. "Come, girls, we've Latin and mathematics to conquer before our excursion."

It was as if she'd thrown a bucket of frigid water on both of them as they wilted and trudged from the breakfast room. Lord Barkley smiled as they walked past, oblivious to the difficulty he'd just caused. He was a kind father, but rather obtuse when it came to managing his children.

He handed Isabelle a purse. "Make sure you purchase something small for the girls—as well as for yourself." He looked at the cap atop her head. "Perhaps a new frippery."

"Thank you, my lord." She took the small pouch and tucked it into her apron pocket where she kept a pencil and scraps of paper.

After a frustrating morning during which the girls could barely contain their excitement and a luncheon at which they ate next to nothing, Isabelle was more than ready to set the girls free. In fact, if she could have sent them along with the dowager and remained behind, she might have done so.

Was that because she was weary after the long morning, or because she was nervous to meet Val's grandmother? Isabelle chose not to answer that and decided to stop asking herself such foolish questions.

Isabelle and the girls waited in the entrance hall for the dowager's arrival. However, when the door opened, it wasn't an older woman who came inside, but a young woman, probably five years Isabelle's junior.

"Good afternoon!" she said brightly from beneath a wide-brimmed hat topped with a cluster of scarlet flowers and an orange feather. Her gown was a pale yellow and flowed from beneath her red pelisse. With vibrant golden hair, sparkling blue eyes, and a bow-shaped mouth, she had to be Val's sister.

"I'm Lady Viola," she said, confirming Isabelle's suspicion. "Grandmama is in the coach—she didn't want to get out only to have to get back in again—but I wanted to come and greet you. I'm so pleased to take you on an excursion today, even if the weather is going to be difficult." By that, Isabelle presumed she meant the rain, which had been falling off and on all day.

Isabelle was secretly delighted to finally meet Val's sister. "We're pleased to meet you. Allow me to present Miss Spelman and Miss Caroline."

Lady Viola looked down at Beatrice, who was only a couple of inches shorter than her, and at Caroline. "It's lovely to make your acquaintance." Then she transferred her warm gaze to Isabelle. "And you must be their governess. Mrs. Cortland, is it?"

Heat rushed to Isabelle's cheeks as she realized she'd forgotten to introduce herself. "Yes." She hastened to curtsey and gave the girls a sharp glance to remind them to do the same.

Beatrice comported herself beautifully, while Caroline lost her balance and had to steady herself lest she fall over.

"Well done!" Lady Viola said. "Shall we be on our way?"

"Yes, please," Beatrice said politely but with an undercurrent of desperate excitement.

The interior of the coach was large, with plush, dark blue velvet seats, but it was still a bit tight for Isabelle and the girls to squeeze together onto the rear-facing seat. The dowager sat on the forward-facing seat, her gaze as keen and assessing as a bird of prey as she surveyed them across the coach.

Once they were situated, Lady Viola, who was next to the dowager, conducted the introductions. "It's too bad the girls are seated, Grandmama, for they demonstrated excellent curtsies."

Caroline shook her head. "I didn't at all. I nearly fell."

Isabelle touched the girl's hand, but before she could whisper in her ear to keep such things to herself, the dowager spoke up. "My girl, you shouldn't say things to denigrate yourself. I didn't ever need to know that your curtsey was lacking—don't ever verbalize your failings. Always hold your head high and comport yourself as if you are the most magnificent person in the world. Still, it's important to master a curtsey." The dowager gave Isabelle a stern look. "You will ensure she practices two dozen times when you return home. Promise me, now."

"I, er, promise."

The dowager narrowed her eyes. "Er? Wherever did you learn to speak?"

"Oxford, Your Grace."

The dowager looked horrified and then disgusted. "You didn't attend Oxford. Do you take me for a fool?"

"My father was warden of Merton College. He educated me personally, Your Grace. Please forgive my...failing a moment ago."

The dowager was quiet a moment, during which Isabelle held her breath. She didn't particularly want to be on Val's grandmother's bad side. Not because she was his grandmother—because really, what did that matter—but because she was one of the most powerful people in Society. On second thought, what did something like that matter to Isabelle?

"You're bold. I like that. Do not disappoint me."

"Ignore Grandmama," Lady Viola said, casting the dowager a look of mock exasperation. "She likes to frighten people." Leaning forward, she smiled at Beatrice and Caroline. "You mustn't let her scare you, because she will like you ever so much more."

The dowager harrumphed.

A few minutes later, they arrived on Bond Street, and their first stop was a linen draper where the dowager planned to select fabric for gowns for herself and Lady Viola. As they departed the coach, the dowager looked down at Beatrice and Caroline. "Do not touch *anything*."

The dowager took her granddaughter's arm and preceded them inside. Caroline leaned toward Beatrice and whispered, "Are you sorry we came yet? If it wasn't for Gunter's, I'd ask to return to His Grace's house."

"Come, girls, don't whisper," Isabelle said, though she couldn't really fault Caroline's grievance.

Once they were inside the shop, any irritation the girls felt faded away as they gaped at the display of silks and muslins and velvets. Isabelle stayed close beside them, afraid Caroline wouldn't be able to help caressing one of the sumptuous fabrics. She also kept an eye on the dowager, whom Lady Viola led to one of the counters. As soon as she situated her grandmother into a chair, she came to Isabelle and the girls.

"Would you like to actually touch some fabric?" Lady Viola asked with a sparkle in her eye.

"Her Grace said we couldn't," Caroline said dejectedly.

"Her Grace doesn't know about the special area." Lady Viola waggled her pale brows. "Come with me." She led them to a back corner of the shop.

Curious, Isabelle followed, eager to see why the area was "special." The answer was soon apparent.

The corner held two boxes: one full of dolls and another of dresses made from fabrics as colorful and rich as those adorning the shop.

Caroline immediately picked up a doll and a dress, then sat in a chair. Beatrice was far more reticent, but Isabelle could see she itched to follow her sister's lead.

Lady Viola seemed to realize this too. She moved to Beatrice's side and spoke in a low tone, but loud enough that Isabelle could hear. "I know you're too old for dolls, but these are for making sample dresses —very small ones. The shop owner puts the dolls and dresses they no longer use over here for their younger clientele. You're welcome to study the gowns to your heart's content."

Beatrice looked up at her, still hesitating, then she glanced toward Isabelle, who gave her a nod of encouragement. Finally, she abandoned her indecision and went to the box of miniature gowns. Withdrawing several, she sat down and sifted through them with care and admiration.

Lady Viola moved to stand next to Isabelle, who thanked her. "How did you know this was here?"

Val's sister shrugged. "A few years ago, I convinced Mr. Broomall to set up this area for all the miserable children who are dragged along with their mothers. It alleviated many things, not the least of which was protecting his inventory from small hands."

"I'm sure he was most eager to adopt your idea."

"It took a bit of persuasion, but eventually, yes." She gave Isabelle a sheepish look. "I can be rather persistent. Just ask my brother."

She didn't have to. Val had told her that Viola was strong-willed and far too clever for her own good. It seemed age had only honed those characteristics. What Isabelle didn't understand was why Lady

Viola was unmarried. She was beautiful, smart, charming, and from one of England's finest families.

It suddenly occurred to Isabelle what Lady Viola had just said, *Ask my brother*. Did she think they were familiar? Worse, did she *know* they'd *been* familiar?

Isabelle wanted to make it clear they were not. "I'm afraid I don't really know His Grace. I don't have much occasion to speak with him."

"I suppose you don't. Pity, he's rather amusing. When he's not arrogant. Actually, sometimes he's amusingly arrogant."

Isabelle laughed before she could stop herself. It was an absolutely apt description, or at least it had been ten years ago. It seemed Val hadn't changed very much. Recovering, Isabelle said, "I didn't mean to laugh. You've simply painted an...*amusing* picture."

"Do you have siblings, Mrs. Cortland?"

Isabelle shook her head. "I do not. You make me regret that."

"If you were to spend time with me and Val —*His Grace*," she said the latter with an exceedingly pompous air, "you may change your mind. We can be rather terrible to each other. But only because we find the other insufferable." She said this with such cheer that Isabelle smiled.

"I don't believe you. It sounds as if you love each other very much." Isabelle also knew that to be true because Val had told her. He'd taken special care to look after his younger sister, especially after their mother had died while he was at Oxford.

"Perish that notion at once, if you please. If Val ever learned someone cared that deeply for him, his head would swell to five times its already gargantuan size." She glanced toward the counter, where the dowager was seated just in time for the older woman to purse her lips in their direction.

With an apologetic sigh, Lady Viola begged Isabelle to excuse her for a moment, then took herself to the other side of the shop, where her grandmother sat perusing fabric. Isabelle watched Beatrice and Caroline as they investigated every single garment in the box. They'd utterly abandoned their restraint and now chattered about the fabrics and the trimmings and how they longed to have such finery.

"Someday we will," Beatrice said firmly. "Mother says I may marry a duke."

"The only duke we've met is His Grace, and he's old." Caroline made a face.

"I haven't met *my* duke yet, silly. I haven't even come out. Anyway, His Grace isn't *that* old, and he's rather handsome, don't you agree?" At Caroline's look of horror, Beatrice rolled her eyes. "Of course you don't. You're only ten and you haven't yet realized...never mind."

Caroline sent her a saucy glance. "That boys— and that includes dukes—are boors? I've known that forever. It's you who haven't worked it out."

Isabelle was torn between laughing at Caroline's combination of naïveté and insight and recoiling at Beatrice's description of Val as handsome. She was far too young to think that, and regardless of what she said, he *was* too old for her.

Nonsense, your father was fourteen years older than your mother, and Val is only sixteen older than Beatrice.

Nevertheless, the thought of such a union made Isabelle ill.

Is that because of the age difference or because he's Val and you've always wanted him for yourself?

There she went asking herself questions again! Isabelle looked toward the counter and saw that the dowager and Lady Viola had finished. The younger woman was helping the older to her feet, then took her arm and guided her toward the door. Lady Viola then exchanged a look with Isabelle, who nodded in response.

"Time to go, girls," Isabelle said.

"Will we get to do any actual shopping?" Beatrice asked with a touch of whine to her tone. "Or did we just come to watch them shop?" She sent a disgruntled look toward the dowager's and Lady Viola's backs as they exited the shop.

"You will get to shop." Isabelle had no idea if that were true, but she was going to do her best to ensure they did. The purse Lord Barkley had given her weighted the pocket of her cloak.

Thankfully, the next stop was a shop where the girls picked out ribbons, and the dowager surprised them all by having it added to her account. "You girls are very well behaved. That is a testament to your governess." The dowager gave Isabelle an approving look.

When they were back in the coach, the dowager asked the girls what they liked to study.

"I like history," Beatrice said.

"I like languages," Caroline said eagerly. "And mathematics. And science."

The dowager looked at Isabelle, a slender gray brow arching. "You teach them science?"

"A bit. Some geology, biology, and astronomy."

Beatrice smiled. "I do love astronomy."

"You are exceedingly well educated," the dowager said to Isabelle. "It's no wonder you're a governess. And yet you are a missus, so I must assume you were wed?"

"I was. My husband passed away six years ago, and I was fortunate to find this position with Lord Barkley's family."

"We're the ones who are fortunate," Beatrice said softly. Isabelle's heart warmed.

"Do you girls have umbrellas?" the dowager

asked, abruptly changing the topic. "It's going to rain by the time we stop again."

"We do not," Isabelle said.

Lady Viola waved her hand. "No matter. Shall we take them to Dalwiddy's, Grandmama?"

"Of course."

A few minutes later, they stopped in front of a shop with an array of parasols and umbrellas. There, the dowager once again purchased umbrellas for the girls, as well as one for Isabelle, who felt odd about accepting such a gift. She'd done so anyway because Lady Viola had silently pleaded with her not to refuse.

Afterward, the rain began in earnest, and they decided to make their way directly to Gunter's. Inside the sweet shop, Lady Viola situated her grandmother at a table, then joined Isabelle and the girls at the counter. Beatrice and Caroline gaped at the array of confections.

"I can't decide what to have," Beatrice said, sounding worried.

Caroline's eyes were wide. "I want one of everything."

"Take your time choosing," Lady Viola said.

The man behind the counter handed Lady Viola a plate of sugar icing drops. She smiled gratefully. "Thank you." Turning to Isabelle, she said, "This is Grandmama's peppermint diavolini. He knows to dish it up as soon as we arrive. I'll be right back."

Isabelle helped Beatrice choose a dish of elderflower ice cream, while Caroline selected an elaborate swan made of spun sugar. Holding her plate with the swan, she looked up at Isabelle. "It's almost too pretty to eat."

"Almost?" Isabelle asked with a smile.

"Oh, I shall eat it." Caroline pressed her lips together with youthful determination and followed her sister to the dowager's table.

Lady Viola returned to Isabelle. "Have you decided what you're going to get?"

"I don't need anything," Isabelle said.

"Oh, come now. You must have something. Even if it's just a bit of diavolini. Grandmama prefers the peppermint, but the chocolate is the best. Don't tell her I said that. You must try some." Lady Viola ordered several pieces, and Isabelle decided there was no point in arguing.

"Papa!" Caroline's excited squeal filled the shop, and Isabelle turned her head to see Lord Barkley enter. He was not alone.

On his heels was the man she'd so desperately needed to avoid.

*V*al took in the image of his sister standing with his former lover, the two looking quite friendly. For a moment, he simply stared at them, wondering what they might be discussing. Isabelle knew all about Viola, but his sister didn't know a thing about Isabelle. And things would likely stay that way.

Barkley went to join his daughters, who sat with Val's grandmother. She appeared to be managing the girls quite well. They sat straight and still and, after Miss Caroline's outburst upon their arrival, spoke quietly.

Walking to the counter just as the man behind it handed a plate of diavolini to his sister, Val plucked up one of the sugary confections and popped it into his mouth. "Delicious." He looked at Isabelle. "Have you ever tried it?"

"Not yet."

"You must." He just barely stopped himself from picking up another and feeding it to her himself. What the hell was he thinking? The answer was simple: that he was ten years younger, back at Oxford the day he'd brought Isabelle a box of confections.

Then he'd kissed her, and she'd tasted even sweeter than the spun sugar flower he'd given her.

That was an exceedingly treacherous line of thought, so he abandoned it at once. "How was shopping?" he asked.

"You know Grandmama," Viola answered, "she bought everyone umbrellas and ribbons for the girls."

A small group of people came into the shop, prompting Val to suggest they sit. He guided them to the table next to his grandmother's, which was already full. He held Isabelle's chair as she sat down, and immediately received a curious glance from Viola. Because propriety said he should have held her chair first. Just as ten years ago, Isabelle quite made him forget common sense.

Before he could help Viola, she'd deposited herself into a chair. "I didn't realize you were meeting us here."

"I decided to accompany Barkley."

The baron, seated at the adjoining table, angled himself toward them. "I told the girls there would be a surprise, but I'm afraid it isn't quite ready, so I brought His Grace instead." He flashed a broad smile at his daughters, as if bringing Val would somehow impress them.

Val could see it did not. Did it, however, impress Isabelle? He sent a surreptitious glance in her direction. She was finally trying one of the diavolini. Lifting a piece, she parted her lips and set it in her mouth, giving him just the briefest glimpse of her tongue.

Grandmama straightened in her chair, as if her ramrod-stiff spine could get any more vertical, while she addressed Barkley. "I was just speaking with the girls in Greek before you arrived, Lord Barkley. They have been well schooled." She sent a staunch look of approval toward Isabelle before returning her hawk-like gaze to the girls. "Now tell me, what are your favorite dances and what instruments do you play?"

Miss Caroline pulled a face that made Val's grandmother suck in her breath. "We haven't learned any of that yet."

Isabelle reached over and gently touched the girl's hand, then leaned to her ear and whispered something. Miss Caroline nodded, then relaxed her features and murmured, "Pardon me."

Grandmama snapped her gaze to Isabelle. "Don't you instruct them on such things? It's past time Miss Spelman began to master a musical instrument."

"I don't teach music or dancing," Isabelle said, folding her hands in her lap.

"I see." Grandmama's disapproval was evident, and Val studied Isabelle for any sign of reaction, but there was none. She was good. Very good. Or perhaps she didn't care what his grandmother thought. Why should she?

Val didn't want Isabelle to feel slighted. "Grandmama, Mrs. Cortland is one of the most highly educated women in England. Her father was well regarded at Oxford."

"Did you know him?"

"He wasn't warden of my college, but I attended a few of his lectures. He was a renowned scholar of Greek literature." It was at one of those lectures that he'd met Isabelle, who'd been seated in the rear dressed as a lad. She'd escaped everyone's notice but Val's. He'd been the last to leave and had seen Isabelle stand. She'd dropped her book and when she'd bent to retrieve it, her hat had fallen off, and he'd seen what she'd attempted to disguise: that she wasn't a young scholar, but a beautiful girl.

"We didn't hire Mrs. Cortland to teach the girls music and embroidery and all of that lady...stuff,"

Barkley said. "That will be handled by someone else." He picked up a piece of Grandmama's diavolini. Val heard Viola's intake of breath and exchanged a look with her. Grandmama didn't share her peppermints with *anyone*.

Barkley brushed his hands together, oblivious to the icy stare Grandmama had directed at him. "Time to leave, girls. I do have that surprise for you at home. Rather, at His Grace's residence. Soon, we *will* be home. Our town house may be ready more quickly than anticipated."

Val rushed to speak before his grandmother called Barkley out about the peppermint. "Because you harass the workers there multiple times a day. One might think my hospitality is lacking."

"Of course not!" Barkley laughed jovially, still unaware of Grandmama's agitation. He looked around at everyone, not just his daughters. "Are we ready, then?"

"I am not," Grandmama said coolly. "But don't let me stop you from leaving." She looked over at Val. "Don't you go, however. My coach will deliver you home."

Barkley stood and ushered his girls to follow suit. "Thank you for your generosity today, Your Grace." He bowed to Val's grandmother, then turned expectantly to Mrs. Cortland, who was rising from her chair. Lord Barkley moved to help her, grazing his hand against her back as she stood.

Val was disappointed to see Isabelle go—this was the only time they'd spent together since that first night. Not that it was the kind of time he wanted to spend with her. He wanted to be alone with her, to discover all the things about her that were different and all the things that were the same. He realized he wanted to go back in time, as if that were possible.

They couldn't, and he'd do best to remember

that. She was a temptation he couldn't indulge, a memory he had to leave behind.

Isabelle stood and dipped a curtsey, despite the closeness of the seating arrangement, toward the dowager. "Thank you, Your Grace." Then she looked toward Viola. "Lady Viola."

Viola smiled broadly at her. "I hope to see you again, Mrs. Cortland."

Barkley and Isabelle departed with the girls, and Grandmama immediately narrowed her eyes at Viola. "Why would you see Mrs. Cortland?"

With a shrug, Viola picked up the last remaining chocolate diavolini. "Perhaps we'll take them shopping again. We should go to Hatchards. I daresay she'd love that. As would the girls."

Yes, Isabelle should go to Hatchards. Why hadn't Val thought of that?

"I don't think we need to take them shopping again," Grandmama said as she reached for her last peppermint. "I've done my favor to Eastleigh, and that is enough."

"You seemed to like them," Viola said with a hint of exasperation.

"That doesn't mean I need to dote upon them. I'm a busy woman, Viola. Besides, their father is a boor." Grandmama pursed her lips in distaste before placing the peppermint in her mouth.

Val turned toward Viola. "How did you find them?"

"Delightful. The girls are curious and charming, and Mrs. Cortland is terribly clever. I should like to welcome her into my circle of friends."

Grandmama let out a soft, nearly inelegant sound. "Your friends are strange."

Viola wasn't the least bit offended by their grandmother's statement. If she and Val took umbrage every time the dowager spoke her mind, they'd spend their lives in a perpetual state of irritation. "One would argue that *I'm* strange, but I know you don't want to hear that."

"You are correct. I do not." She rose, and Val jumped up to help her. "Let us depart. I've correspondence to see to since the weather will not support a jaunt to the park."

When they reached the coach, the footman helped the dowager step up. Val couldn't resist asking his sister, "You found Mrs. Cortland clever?"

"Exceedingly. I wish I'd been educated like she was." There was a wistful quality to her tone. Viola was obsessed with the written word, and had been writing since she'd been old enough to grasp a quill.

"You've done all right, despite Father's insistence that you didn't need to know anything more than needlepoint, dancing, and simpering."

"Simpering was not actually a focus."

He offered her his hand to help her into the coach. "That must be why you're so bad at it."

She gave him a sly, pert smile. "Indeed."

"Would you get in the coach?" Grandmama demanded. "It's freezing."

Inside the coach, Val braced himself for what must come next. He couldn't expect to see his grandmother and not endure an interrogation followed by a lecture.

"What are your marriage prospects, Eastleigh?"

"The same they were last time I saw you, what, four days ago?"

"Don't be saucy with me," she scolded from across the coach as they circled to the other side of the square. "You'll be thirty this year. I understand your reluctance to marry again after that disaster of a first wife, but you're older and wiser now, and you'll choose better. If you'd allowed me to choose the first time—"

Viola put her hand on the dowager's. "If you'll recall, I let you choose *my* husband, and you saw how that turned out."

Grandmama did not appear persuaded by this argument, not that Val expected her to be. They were revisiting old debates. "I still say there was nothing really wrong with him. Even if there was, you would have whipped him into shape—you are my grand-daughter, after all."

Val suppressed a smile. When it came to debate, or anything else, for that matter, Grandmama would never admit defeat.

"What about Lady Penelope?" Grandmama suggested. "She's well-mannered, beautiful, and her lineage is impeccable. She also looks as though you could frighten her with a stare, so I highly doubt you'd encounter any of the same problems you had with That Woman." Grandmama never said Val's wife's name, which was fine with him.

"Grandmama, you frighten *everyone* with your stare, so that's hardly notable," Viola said.

The dowager's lips twitched but she did *not* smile. That would be garish in her opinion. "This is true."

"I'm not even sure I know who Lady Penelope is," Val said. He did, of course, because Cole knew everyone, and as Cole's best friend, Val inevitably ended up knowing everyone too. Not that he *knew* Lady Penelope. He vaguely recalled a fast introduction a week or so ago. But he couldn't be sure.

Grandmama turned the full weight of her disapproval on Val. "If you went to Almack's, you'd know her and many other suitable young ladies. It's Wednesday. We'll go tonight."

He didn't want to go to Almack's tonight or any other night, for that matter. He gave her an apologetic wince. "I already have plans."

"You always have plans."

"I'm an important member of the House of Lords. I chair a committee and—"

She waved her hand, cutting him off. "Next week, then, and I shan't brook a refusal."

Val gritted his teeth but knew better than to argue with her. He'd just ensure something very critical that required his attendance came up. Perhaps he could convince Cole to move up his wedding. To next Wednesday evening.

They'd arrived in front of Grandmama's house several minutes ago, and he was now quite ready to escape further lecture. "I can walk home."

"Don't be silly," Grandmama said. "The coachman will drive you. It's about to rain again."

The footman opened the door, and Val bid his grandmother and sister farewell. The ride to Grosvenor Square took only a few minutes, then he sent the coach right back to Berkley Square.

Val's butler, Sadler, welcomed him home, but the deep crease in his brow said something was amiss. "What's going on?" Val asked without preamble.

"We have additional guests, Your Grace," Sadler said in a low tone as he closed the door.

Val removed his hat and gloves and handed them off to a footman. "Guests plural?"

"Lady Barkley has arrived, and she is not alone."

Whom would she have brought with her? Had something happened to Barkley's son at Oxford? "Is it their son?"

"No, I'm afraid it's a new governess."

Bloody hell. Val immediately wanted to go find Isabelle. Which he absolutely should not. He allowed

logic to tamp his outrage. The girls needed a governess who would teach them—how had Barkley put
it, lady stuff?—the things Isabelle couldn't. That had
to be the new woman's purpose.

Still, he couldn't quite dismiss a lingering feeling
of unease. "We have plenty of room."

"Actually, we do not. The two governesses will
need to share a chamber."

Val recalled the size of Isabelle's room, particularly the narrow bed, which, because he was a lecherous scoundrel when it came to her, had
commanded his attention. "It's not large enough."

"We'll have to make do, sir. We're working on it
now."

"Keep me apprised. I want to see how you
manage—I have grave doubts. In the meantime, I'll
be in my study." Because he couldn't very well seek
Isabelle out.

As Val passed the library, he heard voices through
the half-open door. Angling himself, he peered inside
and saw Barkley leaning against the wall. His face
was pinched and his arms were folded tightly across
his chest, making him appear distinctly uncomfortable.

"It's not fair! I will never like her!" The sound of
a girl bursting into tears rent the air, and Miss Caroline came running from the library, nearly bowling
Val over in her haste. She didn't even pause as she
tore past him.

Her rapid exit had opened the door further, and
now Val could see entirely inside—just as the occupants could see him.

"No, I'll go after her," Lady Barkley said to Isabelle, who had started toward the door. "She's *my*
daughter."

Lady Barkley, a reed-thin woman with prematurely graying hair and a small mouth that was cur rently drawn into a tight moue, strode toward him. The moment she saw him was reflected in the widening of her dark eyes and her sudden stop. She dropped into an awkward curtsey. "Your Grace. Please pardon my daughter's behavior."

"I'm sorry to see she's upset."

Nodding, Lady Barkley thanked him for his concern and moved past him sedately, her shoulders stiff as an overstarched cravat.

Val took in the scene in the library. Barkley had pushed away from the wall, but seemed only more distressed given the lines fanning from his mouth and eyes. Miss Spelman had gone to wrap her arms around Isabelle's waist. An unknown woman—certainly the new governess—stood at the opposite end of the room, her face pale and her hands clasped tightly in front of her. She looked to be a few years older than Isabelle and appeared perhaps even more upset than Barkley. What the hell had happened?

"Beatrice, let Mrs. Cortland go. She's not leaving straightaway."

Isabelle patted the girl's back and bent her head to murmur something in her ear. Miss Spelman nodded, then extricated herself from Isabelle. Tossing a glare toward her father, she turned and started toward the door. Like her mother before her, she offered Val a curtsey before she left.

Barkley sent an apologetic look toward Val. "My apologies for this disruption. Allow me to present our new governess, Miss Shipley." His attention was not on Miss Shipley but on Isabelle.

Miss Shipley dropped into a deep curtsey. "Pleased to make your acquaintance, Your Grace." She kept her gaze directed toward the floor.

"Welcome." Val wanted to throw her and Barkley out so he could have Isabelle to himself. No, he wanted to punch Barkley first. He'd said Isabelle was *leaving*. He'd bloody let her go.

Val got to do none of those things because Isabelle gave him a brief curtsey and murmured, "Please excuse me."

Then she was gone, and Val had to root himself to the floor to keep from following her.

CHAPTER 6

*B*y the time Isabelle reached the third floor, she felt as if she might burst. The anger and hurt and sadness had bound together during her ascent and formed a ball of fire that threatened to burn her from the inside out.

The door to her room was open, and a pair of footmen were attempting to wrestle a second bed into the small space.

"I don't see how it'll fit," the one already inside the room said.

"Has to," the one outside said. "Mr. Sadler was insistent."

"Then let him come do it." The first one sounded rather disgruntled.

Well, no more than Isabelle felt.

Spinning on her heel, she went back the way she came and prayed she wouldn't run into her employers, or worse—the girls. Poor Caroline had been so upset. Isabelle's heart ached for her. She'd grown quite close to both her and Beatrice, and hated that she wouldn't get to see them reach their full potential.

Isabelle swallowed against the ache in her throat. She'd faced and, more importantly, overcome disappointment before. This was not the worst that could happen to her, not the worst that *had* happened to her. She'd clawed her way back from destitution and hopelessness, and she refused to go back.

Thankfully, she encountered no one as she returned downstairs, not until she reached the entry hall. The footman stationed at the door looked in her direction, but she hurried on her way.

Turning to the right, she moved quickly past the library and went to Val's study. Though she'd been here only a few days, she'd made a point of mapping the house so she could better avoid her host. Until now.

Now, she was torn between wanting to find him inside and hoping he was elsewhere so she wouldn't have to suffer the embarrassment of facing him in her current unemployed state.

Why should she be embarrassed? It wasn't her fault Lady Barkley had suddenly decided to hire a new governess. Was it even sudden? For all Isabelle knew, she'd been planning it for some time. Perhaps every "visit" to her "sick" aunt had been an interview for Isabelle's replacement. That thought only rekindled her anger and hurt at being so shockingly dismissed.

Why hadn't the baroness told Isabelle she wanted to replace her? Then Isabelle could have been searching for a new position while Lady Barkley had sought a new governess. For whatever reason, Lady Barkley hadn't wanted to afford Isabelle that courtesy.

The door to the study was ajar, but she had to push it open to go inside. Val looked up from his desk, where he pored over a sheaf of documents stacked before him.

He stood and came around the desk. He was so handsome, even more so than he'd been ten years ago, the faint lines around his eyes giving proof that he still laughed as much as he had when she'd known him.

He stopped short of taking her hands in his, but it was clear he'd been about to. Instead, he dropped them back to his sides. "Isabelle, I'm so sorry about your position."

"I came to see if I could borrow some parchment. And a quill. Well, not borrow the parchment since I plan to write on it and send it away. The quill, however, I shall return. I must also borrow your study so that I may conduct my business. I'm afraid I can't use my chamber as two footmen are currently squeezing another bed inside, and I'd rather stay away from the library in case—"

Abandoning his hesitation, Val took her hand in his, and she was instantly calmed by his warmth and strength. "You still ramble when you're upset."

"When did you ever see me upset?"

He arched a brow at her. "When one of your father's students stole the essay you wrote about Voltaire's *Philosophical Letters on the English*."

She remembered that, of course. Val had understood her outrage. In fact, he'd even taken the matter into his own hands, if memory served. "Didn't you black his eye at the pub that night?"

Grinning, he looked as proud now as he had then. "With glee." His smile faded. "Shall I plant a facer on Barkley? I'd like to."

"As satisfying as that may be, you are no longer the Wicked Duke of Eastleigh. At least I hope you're not. Surely you've matured."

He perched on the front edge of his desk and crossed his arms over his chest. "I thought you liked the Wicked Duke of Eastleigh."

She had—perhaps too much. "His wickedness rubbed off on me. That isn't fair. I was just as…

wicked." She shook her head. "I didn't come here to reminisce. I need to write some letters as I find myself in need of employment."

He winced and gestured toward one of the wing-back chairs angled in front of the hearth, where a low, pleasant fire burned. "Will you sit?"

She didn't want to sit; she wanted to write. First she needed him to provide her the implements she required. Grasping a thread of patience, Isabelle went to the chair and perched on the edge.

Val sat in the other chair, which put their knees only a foot apart. She scooted back on her cushion. His brow shot up, then slowly lowered, indicating he'd noted her movement. Thankfully, he said nothing, though she was more than ready to tell him it was best if they kept their distance.

"I would be happy to frank your letters," he offered. "And please don't tell me you can't accept my assistance. This is an inconsequential thing. Furthermore, I can't imagine you'd want to ask Barkley."

In fact, she'd planned to ask Val to do just that. "Thank you. You're right. I don't want to ask Lord Barkley."

Val scowled. "Why didn't they just hire this additional governess for the things you can't teach them? Surely she isn't as well educated as you and can't possibly tutor the girls in all the subjects you can."

His praise chased away some of her despair. "I made the same argument. However, Lady Barkley said the girls didn't need to learn everything I was teaching them, that it was too much." That might be true, especially to a woman as ill educated as Lady Barkley, but Isabelle feared the real reason she'd been fired was because Lady Barkley was jealous of the close relationship she'd formed with Beatrice and Caroline.

"That's incredibly short-sighted of them. We

shall simply find you a better position. There are far more influential families than Lord Barkley's. My grandmother will ensure you have the finest appointment—"

She cut him off. "No. I do not require, nor do I desire, your grandmother's assistance. It was clear to me she found I lacked certain skills. I highly doubt she'd recommend me as a governess."

He frowned. "Perhaps it's wrong to call you a governess, then. You are a tutor. You could be teaching young men in addition to women."

She didn't disagree, but that wasn't possible. "No one will hire me to teach their sons."

"Have you considered teaching at a school? It's bloody ridiculous you can't teach at Oxford. You're smarter than many of the dons," he added.

She'd done more than consider. She wanted to be headmistress of her own school, and she'd saved nearly enough money to either buy one or start her own within the next year or two. The loss of her employment would set her back, unless she could find another position immediately. Perhaps she ought to accept the dowager's help—if she was willing to offer. Isabelle wasn't as certain as Val, but then she didn't know his grandmother like he did.

And yet, she hated to take another governess position when she'd only plan to leave it in the near future. She'd wondered how she would be able to say goodbye to Beatrice and Caroline, had dreaded it, in fact. Now that the moment was here, she was overcome with sadness. Did she really want to endure that again?

"I can see you're thinking rather deeply," Val said softly. "This must be a blow."

She lifted her gaze to his. "It is what happens, I'm afraid. I do appreciate you dispatching my correspondence."

He exhaled. "I'm glad you'll let me. I am going to offer you something else, and you can't refuse it. You'll move to one of the guest rooms on the second floor."

She wanted to refuse it. She *should* refuse it. "What happens if I decline?"

"As I said, you can't. I'm going to instruct Mrs. Watkins to move your things right now." There was his arrogant streak.

"I should decline."

"You can't. I don't have enough room, and unless you want to share your closet with your replacement, you'll stay in a guest room."

Put like that, he was right. "No, I can't decline," she murmured. She hated not having choices, but then one would think she'd be used to that by now.

He stood. "Help yourself to parchment and quill. The latter is on the desk, and the paper is in the topmost drawer on the left. Just move my documents aside."

"What are they?" she asked, eyeing the desk.

"It's a draft proposal regarding weights and measures. My friend Colehaven is going to present it. His betrothed helped write it."

Isabelle stood and went to the desk. "A woman?"

"She's rather brilliant. In fact, the two of you would get along famously."

Too bad they would never meet. Unless she needed to hire a governess, which she obviously did not since she was not even married yet.

"You remember Cole?" Val asked.

She looked over at him, recalling the two wicked dukes who'd set Oxford on its ear for a time. Some had found them beyond infuriating, but Isabelle's father had liked them both. And of course Isabelle had been utterly captivated by Val. "I do. He's getting married?"

"Yes, soon."

She couldn't help but think of Val's marriage. She'd read about his wedding in the paper right around the time her husband had died. Her relief at being free had been eclipsed by her sadness at learning Val was not. Had she thought she'd had a chance to become his duchess? No, that was absurd. She'd known it then just as she'd known it ten years ago. Just as she knew it now.

"I shall pray that his marriage knows more happiness than either of ours."

Val stepped toward the desk, his gaze dark. "Was your marriage unhappy?"

Yes, but she wasn't going to say so. "I only meant that we lost our spouses rather quickly. That's not a very happy ending."

He stared at her a moment, his eyes intent, before his shoulders relaxed and the tension in his jaw released. Had his marriage been unhappy? She recalled his reaction when she'd first mentioned the death of his wife and longed to ask but didn't dare. Those were intimacies they mustn't indulge.

"I'll see you to your room." He turned to go, then hesitated and pivoted back toward her. "Will you be leaving with Lord and Lady Barkley when their town house is ready?"

"Presumably. He said I could stay as long as necessary, but Lady Barkley strongly suggested I would be able to find something within a fortnight. I took that to mean that I should be gone from their household by then." Perhaps Isabelle's outrage and hurt were also behind her interpretation, but whatever the reason, she planned to exit their household as soon as possible. She'd use her savings to rent lodgings if she had to.

Val's mouth turned down, and his eyes narrowed.

"They won't expel you if you don't have a new situation."

"No, I can't imagine they would." That had been true until today. Until she'd seen the triumph in Lady Barkley's eyes. Then Isabelle had known that the woman wanted Isabelle gone.

"You are welcome to stay here as long as you need."

She stared at him. "And that wouldn't cause a scandal." Her wry tone nearly made him smile.

"I'm sure I can come up with a reason for needing an exceptionally intelligent woman on my staff. Perhaps I'll hire you as my secretary."

"Don't you already have a secretary?"

"I do, but surely I can justify two." He winked at her, and her heart fluttered. For a brief moment, she was tempted to let him take care of her, to fix the wrongs in her world.

But she wouldn't. If she'd learned anything, it was that there was just one person who could be counted on to take care of her: herself.

CHAPTER 7

"*E*astleigh!"

Tonight, Val merely raised his hand in greeting before depositing himself between Cole and Cole's soon-to-be-relative, Thad Middleton. When Doyle brought him his tankard, Val swallowed the contents, then wordlessly handed the empty tankard back to him.

"I haven't seen you drink an ale like that since Oxford." Though Cole's tone was heavy with humor, Val detected the edge of concern.

"Suffice it to say I am dealing with issues I haven't had since Oxford."

Cole's brows lifted for a brief moment before he sipped his beer. Then he rose from his chair. "Pardon us for a bit, Middleton, Eastleigh and I have some Wicked Duke business to discuss." He looked at Val and inclined his head toward the private salon.

Val got up and followed him to the corner table, accepting his refilled tankard from Doyle along the way.

"Now what's wrong?" Cole asked as soon as he was seated.

"Barkley hired a new governess to replace Isabelle."

Cole winced. "That's bloody awkward. He couldn't have waited until he was out of your house?"

"Apparently not. As you can imagine, we are full to the brim with all of them and the staff they traveled with. Isabelle is now ensconced in a guest room next to my chamber." Val peered at Cole over the rim of his mug before he took a drink.

"That sounds...convenient."

"It was that or cram the new governess into her tiny room along with her. What would have been uncomfortable in a normal circumstance would then have been utterly disagreeable. Can you imagine having to share a closet-sized chamber with the person who'd stolen your job?"

"I presume she didn't *steal* it—"

Val glowered at him and was satisfied when Cole didn't finish his ridiculous and unnecessary observation.

"You are quite upset by this," Cole said.

"Shouldn't I be? Isabelle is the smartest woman I know. If there's a better governess out there, on second thought, no, there isn't a better governess out there. There are just different kinds. So she doesn't play an instrument or teach them other...lady stuff. Barkley could have hired this new governess in addition to Isabelle."

"Have you pointed that out to him?"

Val snapped his gaze to Cole's. "No. Should I?" He waved a hand. "Never mind. It's probably curious enough that I am lodging her in a guest room. If I speak to Barkley on her behalf, I am confident she would not appreciate it. As it was, I had to force her to move into the guest room, and if she hadn't been faced with having to share with her replacement, I'm not sure she would have agreed."

"Force her? I hope you're not being an arrogant ass."

"I am not. I am simply trying to help a friend in need."

"A *friend*. Who is sleeping in the chamber next door. Are you going to behave yourself?"

"I must. She's made it clear she is not interested in resurrecting the past. She is completely focused on finding new employment. You know everyone—who is in need of a governess?"

Cole cupped his hands around his mug. "Just to clarify, one that doesn't teach, what was it you said—lady stuff?"

"Will that be a terrible hindrance?"

Cole shrugged. "What do I know of it? I'll see what I can find out."

Someone yelled "Eastleigh" from the main salon, and it was followed by a chorus of laughter. Both Val and Cole turned their heads in that direction.

"Is someone impersonating you?" Cole asked. "It sounds like you just came in, but they all know you're back here."

"Let's investigate." Val stood, and Cole followed him back to the main salon.

"Eastleigh." Middleton waved them over, and they took the seats they'd recently vacated.

"Jack has just come from Brooks's with some news."

Jack sat next to Cole, his tankard already in front of him. "You know I don't truck in gossip or follow the foolish wagers at White's. However, I was at a meeting at Brooks's when I heard mention of a new wager and felt certain you would want to know." He looked straight at Val. "Now that Colehaven is to be wed, you are apparently the most sought-after bachelor of the Season. Someone wagered you will be next to wed."

"Who would take that bet?" Middleton asked. "The wagerer is an imbecile."

"At last count, there are at least a dozen wagers." Jack cast a sympathetic eye toward Val. "You will undoubtedly be besieged at the very next Society event you attend."

"It's to be a sport, then." Middleton shook his head. "Barbarous."

"I determined it was better to warn you," Jack said.

"Thank you?" Val contemplated a trip to Scotland. Or perhaps India. Maybe Australia. Yes, living with convicts might be preferable to the circus he was about to be subjected to.

"You may never attend a Society event again," Cole murmured. "But you're not missing my wedding or the breakfast."

Of course he wouldn't. "I'll come in disguise."

Cole grinned. "Please do. That would amuse Diana greatly."

"It would not amuse my grandmother. None of this will."

"Has she given up on pressuring you to wed again?" Cole asked.

"Not at all. In fact, she's redoubled her efforts. But you know how she is about notoriety. She won't like it, and I pity the gentlemen who placed those wagers if they are ever in Grandmama's vicinity."

Cole shivered. "Indeed." He took a drink of beer as the conversation around them moved to other topics. Keeping his voice low, he said, "You do plan to marry again, don't you? I realize we've never definitively discussed it, but given the title and your responsibilities—"

"You're really going to lecture me about ducal responsibilities?"

"There's no call to be obnoxious. I know this is a sensitive subject, as it should be. My apologies."

"No need to apologize," Val muttered. Because

Cole was right. Again. Val did have responsibilities, which meant he had to marry again. The mere thought of it turned his blood to ice and made his insides swirl with nausea.

Logically, he knew the likelihood of him marrying another woman like Louisa was nearly impossible. But sometimes logic was overpowered by base emotions like fear and self-doubt. He'd chosen Louisa of his own free will. And it had been the worst mistake of his life.

Would he marry again? Yes, right about when the gates of Hell were coated with ice.

∼

*I*f yesterday's lessons had been challenging due to the girls' excitement about their impending shopping trip, today's were positively painful. Between the awkwardness of Isabelle sharing her duties with Miss Shipley and the girls' overwhelming sadness and anger—Beatrice was more sad, while Caroline was petulant with anger—it was a truly excruciating way to spend a morning.

After lessons in science and Latin, during which Miss Shipley was unable to keep up with either, Isabelle turned the teaching over to the older woman, who introduced both girls to wielding a needle. They removed from the table to a seating arrangement near the hearth, where a cozy fire heated the large room.

Seated in a chair angled toward a settee on which Isabelle sat between the girls, Miss Shipley opened a basket and pulled out three embroidery hoops fitted with fabric. After passing one each to Beatrice and Caroline, she returned to the basket and withdrew needles and thread. She looked to Isabelle. "I'm afraid I don't have a fourth hoop."

"That's quite all right," Isabelle said, feeling relieved. Perhaps she could excuse herself from this lesson entirely.

Caroline crossed her arms over her chest and sent Miss Shipley a mutinous glare. "I don't want to embroider." On second thought, Isabelle decided she should stay.

"Perhaps you can just watch today," Miss Shipley said kindly.

Isabelle felt sorry for the woman. None of this was her fault. She'd been hired to do a job, and she was simply trying to do it.

"I'll try it," Isabelle said, hoping to bolster Miss Shipley's confidence and show Caroline that embroidery wasn't so bad.

Ten minutes and several stab wounds later, Isabelle revised her opinion. Embroidery had clearly been created by the devil himself. She could mend a tear or sew a button, but jabbing a needle into fabric for the purpose of creating a design was clearly beyond her.

Miss Shipley unraveled the second knot Isabelle had created and handed the hoop back to her. "Just take it slow. Once you master a single stitch, the rest will fall into place."

Right now, mastering a single stitch seemed as achievable as sitting in the House of Lords. Still, Isabelle would persist. It was important for the girls to know they shouldn't give up in the face of adversity. Or killer needles.

"I did it!" Beatrice exclaimed, presenting her row of perfect stitches to Isabelle.

Smiling, Isabelle glanced toward the new governess, who looked over at them with something akin to envy. "Show Miss Shipley," Isabelle told Beatrice.

Beatrice presented her embroidery to Miss Shipley, but had lost some of the ebullience she'd displayed a moment ago. It was going to take time for them to welcome the new woman into their lives. Isabelle only hoped Miss Shipley would be patient. So far, she believed that would be the case.

Turning to Caroline, who was seated beside her, Isabelle asked if she wanted to try.

Caroline shook her head. "No. Embroidery is boring. And dangerous. Your finger is still bleeding."

Isabelle looked down and saw there was now a small red dot on the fabric. She winced and sent an apologetic look toward Miss Shipley.

"How are things going this morning?" Lady Barkley swept into the library and glided to stand between Miss Shipley's chair and the settee. "Embroidery lessons, how splendid." As she looked over the settee, she frowned. "Why aren't you sewing, Caroline?"

"I don't want to." Caroline didn't even try to erase the bitterness from her tone.

"Caroline, you will cease that attitude this instant." Lady Barkley turned her attention toward Miss Shipley. "Why is Mrs. Cortland sewing and Caroline is not?"

Miss Shipley stared up at the baroness and seemed to have difficulty forming words. Isabelle jumped to the rescue. "When Caroline demonstrated her reluctance to try it, I thought I would show her how pleasing it could be."

"Only you didn't because you keep making knots, and you've bled all over it." Tears swam in Caroline's eyes, and Isabelle had to stop herself from wrapping the girl in a tight hug. She would've done it if Lady Barkley wasn't standing there staring at them in stern disapproval.

"It looks as though I've come at just the right time to suggest a walk. Come, girls, your hats and gloves are in the hall." Lady Barkley pursed her lips at Isabelle, her gaze lingering on the bloodstained handkerchief in her lap. "Perhaps you should stay and work on your needle skills."

Torn between wanting to spend as much time with Beatrice and Caroline as possible and relief at not having to suffer Lady Barkley—when had the woman become her enemy?—Isabelle succumbed to relief. "I'll do that, thank you."

"Should I come too?" Miss Shipley asked.

Lady Barkley looked at the new governess as if she were daft. "Of course."

Miss Shipley stood with alacrity, and Beatrice followed suit. She cast Isabelle a sad look that squeezed her heart.

Lady Barkley delivered her youngest an expectant stare. "Caroline?"

Rising with great reluctance, Caroline pushed out a frustrated breath. Isabelle gave the girl's hand a squeeze and offered an encouraging smile. Still looking dejected, Caroline marched from the room.

As soon as they were gone, Isabelle set her ruined embroidery on Miss Shipley's basket. She had no intention of working on needlepoint when she needed to find a job.

Instead, she went up to her room, a beautifully decorated chamber with a four-poster bed, an armoire and a dresser, a wide, warm hearth, and the best part: a desk. She would draft more inquiries today.

As she traversed the gallery toward her chamber, she encountered Lord Barkley, who greeted her with a warm smile, as if he hadn't just turned her world upside down the day before. "You didn't accompany Lady Barkley and the girls on their walk?"

"No, that's Miss Shipley's duty now," she said coolly.

He winced. "Damn me. I regret how all this happened. I didn't realize Lady Barkley was going to arrive with a new governess in tow."

"You weren't aware she was going to hire someone to replace me?"

"She's been threatening it for some time—interviewed several candidates—but I admit I didn't think she'd actually do it. You're quite accomplished, and the girls adore you." He glanced beyond her along the gallery and lowered his voice. "In truth, I am trying to convince Lady Barkley to keep you on. Why can't the girls have two governesses? It only makes sense."

Yes, it did, but given the animosity Lady Barkley now freely showed toward Isabelle, it seemed sense might not emerge the victor. "I do appreciate your support, my lord."

He took her hand in his. "You shall always have it. It is not just the girls who will be bereft by your departure." He ran his thumb along the back of her hand, and though it was a slight movement, it changed everything. What he said next only confirmed her fear. "It would be my pleasure to ensure you are well cared for."

That was a proposition. Had he always felt that way about her? Had Lady Barkley realized it and decided to replace Isabelle? She felt sick.

Snapping her hand away from his, she resisted the urge to wipe it on her apron. "I have always cared for myself, my lord, and will continue to do so. My welfare is no longer your concern."

She pushed past him and strode straight to her room, where she shut the door and engaged the lock for good measure. Shaking, she made her way to the desk and sank onto the chair.

How could she stay for the remainder of the fortnight? It was already torture to be with the girls, seeing their sadness and knowing their time together was finite. Now it would also be torture knowing Lord Barkley looked at her in a different light, and that Lady Barkley likely knew it.

What a tangle!

She had to find a job—any job—immediately. There had to be something she could do, even temporarily. She *had* always cared for herself, and she *would* continue to do so.

Armed with resolve and courage, she grabbed her things and went in search of freedom.

CHAPTER 8

It became evident that Isabelle should have dedicated far more time and enthusiasm toward needlework. If she had, she might have obtained employment in a millinery shop sewing hats or stitching dresses for a modiste. Instead, she found herself standing at the back door of a tavern that was apparently in dire need of a barmaid. The pie seller at the end of the street had pointed Isabelle in this direction after she'd inquired about any jobs in the area.

Taking a deep breath, she knocked on the door. After several moments with no answer, she lifted her hand to knock again just as the portal opened.

"Delivery?" the woman asked, wiping her hands on her apron.

"I'm inquiring about a position for a barmaid," Isabelle said, thinking she'd never imagined herself saying those words. But desperation called for drastic measures.

The woman, who seemed about Isabelle's thirty years, looked her up and down. "Do you have experience?"

"Er, no." Isabelle thought of how the dowager would have cringed at her vocalization, but then decided her speech would pale compared to her situation, which would have horrified Val's grandmother.

And what would Val think of her working as a barmaid?

Isabelle stiffened. She refused to let his or his grandmother's opinions—or anyone else's—dictate her life. She'd always done what she must to survive, and she would continue to do so.

As the silence stretched while the woman studied Isabelle, rejection seemed imminent. Isabelle was about to turn when the woman said, "Well, you look reliable. Are you reliable?"

"Very. And I can start immediately."

The woman's face lit, and she grinned. "You should have started with that. I need someone tomorrow. In fact, if you can come in now, I'll give you a tour and get you situated so you can start right up tomorrow."

It was exactly what she needed, if not what she wanted. "Show me what I need to know."

The woman held the door open and beckoned her inside. "I'm Prudence. Welcome to the Wicked Duke."

The…Wicked Duke? It couldn't be. He wouldn't own a tavern. He was a duke.

"I'm Mrs. Isabelle Cortland. Pleased to make your acquaintance."

Prudence led her through a passageway into the kitchen, then turned and narrowed an eye at Isabelle. "You don't sound like our usual barmaid, but then you said you aren't a barmaid. What are you, exactly?"

"A governess until recently."

"Well, you'll fit right in here. We get all kinds in the Wicked Duke—blacksmiths, members of Parliament, barristers, vicars, dockworkers, even dukes."

Prudence chuckled. "Well, the two dukes who own the place, anyway."

Isabelle swallowed as unease flitted through her. "Two…dukes own this tavern?"

Prudence nodded. "Colehaven and Eastleigh, but don't let them intimidate you. They're as normal and friendly as anyone."

Eastleigh.

Isabelle should politely decline the position and keep looking. Except she'd been looking for hours, and this was the only thing she'd found. She needed to get away from Barkley before he took an uncomfortable moment and made it into something far worse. What did he have to lose since she was on her way out?

No, she couldn't walk away from this. That Val owned the place was an even better reason to take the job. She knew it would be well run and, most importantly, safe. As safe as any tavern *could* be.

"Tomorrow is one of our biggest days of the year," Prudence said, drawing Isabelle from her concerns. "We celebrate St. Valentine—both the actual saint and the Duke of Eastleigh, since he is named after the saint. That's why we need you so badly." Prudence smiled at her. "Are you ready to become acquainted with the Wicked Duke?"

Isabelle choked back a laugh. Oh, she was plenty acquainted with a wicked duke. And what would he say when he learned she was his newest employee?

She ought to tell him, but suspected he might not like it. Which was ironic since he'd offered to help her—an offer she'd vehemently declined, and yet here she was in his employ. This was different, she reasoned. This was a job, and he hadn't hired her.

Hopefully, she'd find something else, but in the meantime, this would have to do. She hoped Val would understand.

~

*D*espite his desire to stay away from all Society events, Val found himself at a ball that very evening. He hadn't wanted to go—because of the wager—but he knew he couldn't withdraw from Society completely. His position in the Lords required at least a modicum of social engagement, and then there was his grandmother. If he didn't demonstrate at least a half-hearted attempt to feign interest in finding a wife, she'd never let him alone.

Unfortunately, his pretense, for that was precisely what it was, would only encourage the wagers and, in turn, the matchmaking mamas. To avoid being announced, he slipped into the Mortrams' ballroom from an adjoining salon. Nevertheless, he was set upon almost instantly as young misses eyed him while not so subtly dangling their dance cards.

Val ignored the lot of them while he searched for the dowager. She was seated across the ballroom, naturally, and it was some time before Val was able to reach her.

Viola stood beside her, a cheerful smile lifting her lips. "Good evening, Val. You stole into the ballroom like a thief."

"Why would you do that?" Grandmama asked crossly. "Never mind. I hope you won't do it again."

"It seems I've gained a bit of notoriety." Val was all too aware of people staring at him—more than normal.

"You're always notorious," Viola said unhelpfully. "Or at least popular. Everyone wants to talk with you or dance with you. Or marry you," she added with a teasing giggle. She'd obviously heard about the wagers.

He gave her a look that promised retribution, and she merely batted her eyes in faux innocence.

If she knew about the wagers, Grandmama did too.

"Of course he's popular," the dowager said. "He's Eastleigh. Do you know how many women would love to be your duchess? Particularly after the last one —they're all desperate to prove that you deserve a better wife."

Val wasn't sure that was true at all, but he wasn't going to debate her. It wasn't worth debating her on *most* things. However, the time was coming when he'd have to tell her the truth, that he wasn't ready to marry again and didn't know when he would be.

Besides, he was still young. Plenty of gentlemen didn't marry until they were well into their thirties. His friend Jack Barrett wouldn't even contemplate marriage until he was thirty-five. That was simply the way it was done in his family—attain professional success and then wed. Jack was currently gaining political momentum, and Val fully expected him to be appointed to the government when the Whigs took power.

Val might not be as deep into things as Jack, but he took his position very seriously. "Grandmama, I'm far too busy to spend time searching for a wife. There are simply too many issues facing the country that must be addressed."

"I can't argue that, especially after what happened to Prinny. Some people are so uncivilized."

"Which is precisely why I'm needed and my focus must be elsewhere." The prince had left Westminster after opening Parliament and someone had shot at his coach, breaking the window. With the Spenceans and other radical groups gathering and causing upheaval, it was not an exaggeration for Val to say they were very busy in the House of Lords.

"Balderdash. It's precisely because of all that distress that you should have a wife at home."

Viola gave a tiny shake of her head, silently warning Val to drop it. As if he didn't know when to back away from their grandmother.

"Do you know what would be nice?" Val asked.

Grandmama's gray brows pitched to a drastic angle. "What's that?"

"If you would take half the energy you spend harassing me about a wife and direct it at Viola. At least I actually married. It's her turn to wed."

Viola gave him a self-satisfied smile. "Too bad I'm so far back on the shelf, no one can reach me."

"I'd be happy to give you a push."

"Stop behaving like infants," Grandmama snapped. "Eastleigh, humor me and dance with one young lady tonight. One won't kill you."

He exhaled in resignation. "Fine, but don't ask me to go to Almack's next week."

Grandmama glowered at him. "You already promised." She looked toward Viola. "You heard him."

"Actually, he didn't." She tossed a look tinged with apology that was certainly meant to atone for her earlier taunt.

Val inclined his head with appreciation.

After satisfying his grandmother's request to dance with one young lady, Val left the ball. He'd planned to go to the Wicked Duke but found he didn't particularly feel like company. There'd simply been too much talk of marriage, and that never failed to raise the specter of Louisa. Even in death, she plagued him.

As he strode along the gallery toward his chamber, he slowed when he reached Isabelle's door. He lingered for a moment, knowing she was just on the other side of a rather thin panel of wood. She was so close and yet utterly untouchable.

He continued on and went into his chamber,

where he stripped away his coat and cravat and deposited them in his dressing room for his valet to deal with later. Moving to the sideboard where he kept a bottle of brandy, he poured a glass and closed his eyes as he lifted it to take a sip.

A light rap on his door arrested his movement, the glass stalled in midair on the way to his lips. He turned his head, wondering who would knock on his door at this hour even as his pulse began to pick up speed.

He set the glass down and went to the door. He barely had it open before Isabelle ducked inside. His heart rate increased so that he was sure she would hear it pounding a frantic rhythm. For her.

Words failed him. He was too surprised that she'd come here after her concerns about their past association coming to light. Association? He nearly laughed at the absurdity of that inadequate term.

"I'm sorry to bother you," she said, taking a position near the door. Her light brown hair hung in a thick, single plait over her right shoulder, and she wore a simple dressing gown with a high neck, the modesty of which did nothing to quell his rising desire. "I wanted to speak with you as soon as possible. I've found a job, and I'm leaving in the morning."

His hopes for the reason for her visit crumbled to dust. She was leaving? "Where are you going?"

She fidgeted with the edge of her long sleeve. "I think it's probably best if I don't say."

"And yet you came here to tell me." He frowned as dissatisfaction swirled through him. This was not how things were supposed to be between them. How were they supposed to be, then?

"Perhaps I shouldn't have." She pivoted toward the door but didn't move toward it. "I thought... I wanted to say goodbye before I left. I didn't think I'd see you in the morning."

He moved, not to block her, but to put himself in her line of sight. "I'm glad you did. I can't help thinking there's a reason we encountered each other again."

Her gaze met his, and in the bright blue depths, he saw myriad emotions, none of which he could define. Her brow arched in that arousing fashion, and Val was suddenly aware of their location and the proximity of his bed. "You think Fate brought us together?" she asked with a sardonic edge.

He lifted a shoulder and edged toward her. "Unfinished business between us, maybe."

"Perhaps we did need to see each other. Whatever the reason, I am glad to have had your support with what's happened."

Need—he wasn't sure about that. But want? He wanted her more now than he had ten years ago. Which was silly. He barely knew the woman she was today, but he could see that she still cared for those around her, that she possessed a fierce independence, and that she did things on her terms, as much as a woman could. He suddenly envied her freedom.

"Are you certain there's no other reason you came to see me tonight?" He wanted so badly to kiss her, to see if the spark between them still burned.

"I—" She pressed her lips together, and her eyes glinted with determination. "Yes. I'd like to kiss you goodbye."

"Just kiss me?" This was how that one night had started, with a single kiss to say goodbye. Then passion had swept them away. Ten years on, surely he knew better. But given the way his cock was hardening, perhaps not.

A faint blush crept up her face. "I shouldn't have presumed." She stepped forward, her focus moving to the door.

Val put himself in front of her and lifted his

hand to gently touch her temple, brushing a way-ward curl behind her ear. "You could never be pre-sumptuous. Not with me. Whatever you want, I would freely give."

"Then kiss me. One last time."

Though he could listen to those words in a chorus every day for the rest of his life, he wouldn't make her say it again. Closing the small distance be-tween them, he wrapped his arms around her and touched his lips to hers. Her hands came up to his shoulders, clutching his waistcoat and making him wish he'd removed more of his clothing.

The scent and taste of her was so familiar. He'd never been able to smell lilies without thinking of her.

He let her control the kiss—she'd asked for it, and he would be her servant. She curled her hands about his neck, the warmth of her fingertips heating his nape and scalp, reminding him of a night so un-paralleled that it sometimes hurt to think of it. Par-ticularly after what he'd endured with Louisa.

No, he wouldn't think of her, wouldn't allow her to sully this moment. Or any moment ever again.

Isabelle's tongue stroked his lip, and a wave of desire washed over him. He met her quest, touching his tongue to hers as she deepened the kiss. And then they were lost, cast upon a sea of memory and dis-covery as their bodies pressed together.

This was the dream he'd nurtured for ten long years given form and substance. It was a new dream he'd nurture for another decade. The thought of that —of what she'd said, "one last time," drove him to claim perhaps more than he should. He moved a hand down to her backside, pulling her flush against him.

She responded by nipping his lip and kissing him again. And pressing her pelvis to his. Her heat caressed his erection, and it was all he could do to keep from sweeping her into his arms and bearing her to the bed.

Val unsealed his mouth from hers. Their shortened breaths filled the air. He pressed his forehead to hers and caressed her spine, her nape, her hip. "Stay with me, Isabelle."

"That's what you said to me then," she whispered.

"I know. I am as seduced by you now as I was then."

She brought her hand up and touched his face, her palm pressing against his cheek. Her gaze was steady as her lips curved into a sultry smile. "As I am by you." She touched her lips to his, but it was brief. And then she stepped back.

"As tempted as I am, I have to go."

"If you ever need me, I am here. Always."

She nodded, then stepped around him and slipped from his room.

From my life. Again.

Maybe she'd appear again in another ten years.

$\mathcal{T}$here were at least a half-dozen Valentine's Day balls in town, but one of the most popular events on this romantic day was the so-called Feast of St. Valentine at the Wicked Duke. It was Val's favorite day of the year for two reasons. The first was because everyone called it "his" day and referred to him as his namesake, St. Valentine.

This year's feast would be their most ornate yet, and Cole had crafted yet another Valentine beer. Val only hoped he'd brewed enough as they'd run out the last two years running.

Val arrived to a chorus of "St. Valentine!" instead of Eastleigh, which the pub's denizens called him only on this day. In fact, they wouldn't just keep their exclamations of his name to his entry, they would shout it out all night at odd intervals as met their fancy.

The main salon, decorated with handmade valentines and clusters of flowers, was sparsely populated since it was still early evening. Those that were already here were the stalwart anti-romantics. That most of the attendees came to this event precisely because they were either not in love or steadfastly avoiding the emotion was the point of the event—

celebrating the absence of love and the freedom that brought.

That was usually the second reason it was Val's favorite day.

But today it was not. Today, all he could think about was love—or something akin to love—lost.

No, not love. Whatever he felt for Isabelle, it wasn't that.

He needed a night of revelry and abandon. A night of friends and Cole's beer.

"I'll be back in a few hours," Cole said after quickly greeting Val.

"Back? Where are you going?"

"To Lady Donnell's ball." Cole blinked at him. "I told you I was going."

Val vaguely recalled that. "I didn't think you were serious. How can we have our Feast of St. Valentine if you aren't here?"

"I *will* be here, just later. I need to go waltz with my bride." He stared at Val in question. "You know what Valentine's Day is actually for, don't you?"

Val grunted. "Love is making you boring."

"Love is making me happy." Cole grinned to further annoy Val. "You should try it again some time."

Before Val could swear at him, Cole ducked away and left the tavern. Val went to the bar, and Doyle slid him his tankard full of Cole's Valentine Ale. "He made an adjustment to it this year. Something his betrothed suggested."

Of course he did. Scowling, Val picked up his mug and took a sip. It was, of course, maddeningly good.

He took a deeper drink and silently chastised himself. He wouldn't begrudge Cole his happiness—he deserved every bit of it.

"A new barmaid started today," Doyle said. "Normally, we wouldn't have her start on a night like this, but with Gertie sick, we were desperate."

"Excellent, thank you. I'll just go check on things in the kitchen." Val strode to the rear of the tavern and into the kitchen, where cooks were bustling here and there. It smelled delicious, and he wondered if he might find a spare piece of ham or beef somewhere.

As he pivoted toward a worktable, a woman came from his left and ran square into him, spilling a jug of wine down his front.

The damp soaked all the way through his shirt, and he looked down at the deepening burgundy stain covering his coat, waistcoat, shirt, and cravat. "Bloody hell!"

"Val?" Still clutching the jug, Isabelle looked up at him, her blue eyes narrowing as she winced.

"Isabelle? What the devil are you doing here?"

Her apparent discomfort increased as she hugged the jug to her chest as if it were some sort of shield. "I'm the new barmaid."

He was keenly aware of the silence that had fallen over the kitchen as everyone stopped their work and stared at them. Without thought, he took the jug from her hands and placed it on the nearest surface. Then he clasped her elbow and pulled her from the kitchen.

"What are you doing?" she asked, trying to tug her arm from his grip.

He tightened his hold, careful not to hurt her. "Come with me. Please."

"Let go of me."

He did as she asked and paused, staring at her. They stood in the storage room, surrounded by foodstuffs and implements for cooking and cleaning. "You can't work here."

She crossed her arms over her chest, her eyes

blazing. "You're going to terminate my employment too?"

Hell and the devil. He couldn't very well do *that.* "Of course not, but Isabelle, this is my pub. Obviously, you know that." He scowled. "Is that why you wouldn't tell me anything last night?"

She lifted a shoulder and glanced away. "I was—am—in desperate need."

"To work as a barmaid? This is far beneath you." She should be tutoring the best families in the realm. Or running Oxford. That would never happen, although she bloody well could.

"It's honest work." She looked him up and down, but there was nothing provocative about her appraisal. "Owning and operating a tavern apparently isn't beneath *you.*"

"I'm not working *in* the tavern."

She cocked her head to the side. "I could have sworn Prudence showed me your office where you and Colehaven have desks."

Val muttered an oath. "I told you I would help you—whatever you require."

"And I told you I can't accept anything from you."

"But you can work for me? How is that different from just taking my money?"

Her jaw dropped again. "Are you in earnest? This is completely different from taking your money. As I said, this is honest work."

"And my giving you money would be a transaction between friends. A *secret* transaction no one ever need know about. You could even call it a loan if you prefer."

She stared at him as if he'd just offered to steal everything she owned instead of give her money. "You're mad."

"Perhaps, but only because I care about you.

Barkley will be gone in a few days, and you can come and stay with me for as long as you need."

She blew out a breath in disgust. "If you truly cared about me, you'd see how scandalous that would be. Everyone would assume I was your mistress, and I can't very well become a headmistress after that."

Headmistress? "Are you going to be a head-mistress?"

She uncrossed her arms and threw them in the air in frustration. "Someday, I hope. The point is, you'll narrow my options if you try to provide for me in any way."

"And I would argue that working as a barmaid in a notorious tavern will also narrow your options."

"My future employer, whoever it may be, needn't ever know."

"Your future employer could be sitting in the main salon right now. Or his brother. Or his neighbor. Your employment would not be secret." Neither would her staying with him. She was right—it was a foolish and scandalous idea. There had to be another way. A way she would accept.

The fire in her eyes had diminished a bit, but the taut set of her mouth and the tension of her shoulders told him she was still annoyed. He didn't want her to be annoyed with him. "I'm sorry," he said, inhaling to calm his racing pulse. "I was just surprised to see you here."

"I should have told you."

"Let us find a solution." He tried to sound helpful. "You must agree you can't work here."

She recrossed her arms in front of her. "I could work in the kitchen."

"I have a better idea, and I hope you won't be too stubborn to accept it."

"I am not stubborn." The picture she presented —arms crossed, brow creased, mouth pulled into a severe line, body stiff, chin jutting—was the very definition of stubborn.

Val fought a smile. In addition to how she looked, saying you weren't stubborn in the midst of an argument where you refused to yield was akin to saying you weren't hungry when your belly rumbled. "So you don't stay up all night deciphering riddles anymore?"

She blinked as if he'd thrown her off-kilter for a moment. "I haven't found one that I couldn't solve in quite some time."

"But if you did, you wouldn't stop until you finished it. You wouldn't surrender."

She lifted her chin, which gave her a haughty air. "Surrender leads to disappointment."

Surrender had led them to each other. Attraction. Temptation. Surrender.

Finally, a plan came to him, and it was brilliant. Or nearly so. "I promise you my idea will not disappoint you. Move in with my grandmother and Viola as Viola's chaperone."

One of her eyes narrowed. "Doesn't your grandmother fulfill that role?"

"Yes, but she isn't as spry as she once was. There are things Viola wants to do that Grandmama can't, so Viola needs a chaperone." She didn't either. Viola did as she pleased and didn't give a fig what anyone thought.

Isabelle pursed her lips as she regarded him in silence for a moment. Despite the tension between them, she looked eminently kissable, and it was hard not to recall her mouth on his. Had that been only last night?

One of the cooks ducked into the storage closet to grab something, breaking the spell that had begun to weave itself over him. "Beg your pardon," she murmured before dashing back out.

Isabelle lowered her arms to her sides. "Why do I think being Viola's chaperone is an unnecessary job?"

"It *is* necessary. You'll be doing us a favor. You like Viola, don't you?"

"I do. Your grandmother may not like me, however."

"Bah, her bark is worse than her bite. She likes you fine." He took a step toward her. "Come, this is an excellent solution. Surely you can see that."

"You are as arrogant and managing as ever." She was not going to give up easily. Maybe she wasn't going to give up at all.

"And you are more stubborn than I ever realized. You need help. This is a way I can provide it without causing you harm."

She took a deep breath, her chest rising and falling. "Do they know about me? About us?" Her voice was low, and the timbre of it set his blood afire.

"Of course not."

She glanced away and worried her lower lip before looking back at him. "I hate being in a corner. But I've been in them before and found my own way out. I prefer to make my own choices."

His patience was wearing thin. "You want choices? Stay at my house or stay at my grandmother's, but you are not working in my pub."

"So you *would* dismiss me?"

"To give you a better job, yes." He held his hands up, pleading with her. "For the love of God, Isabelle, take my help! I am not your enemy."

She stared at him, and he held his breath, his brain scrambling to think of other ways to persuade her, to make her see reason. "Fine, I'll go to the dowager's. If she's agreeable. But if she's not, you'll let me work here in the kitchen."

"She'll be agreeable." If she wasn't, Val would

make her that way. "I'll take you there now. Where are your things?"

"Behind you, actually. I brought them here until later, when I'd planned to stay with Prudence until I find my own room to let."

She was going to sleep in Cheapside? He was glad she'd found a job here and not somewhere questionable. "It's lucky you came here. I'd say Fate is wielding her hand once again."

"Who said the luck was good?" She moved past him and picked up her two valises. "I suppose you wish to leave now?"

"You won't regret this, Isabelle. This will give you the time and opportunity to find an appointment that suits your knowledge and talent."

"And you'll leave me alone?" she asked.

"I will." Though it pained him greatly. Seeing her here had only served to prove how much he'd hated saying goodbye to her last night. He wasn't sure he could do it again. And yet, what was the alternative?

"Promise me."

He looked her in the eye. "I promise." He uncrossed his fingers and took the valises from her hand.

~

After driving to Grosvenor Square so Val could change his wine-soaked clothing, during which time Isabelle had waited in the coach, they arrived at the dowager's house in Berkeley Square. What the house lacked in size compared to Val's, it more than made up for in opulence. The art crammed into the entrance hall alone was enough to enchant Isabelle and convince her this wasn't a bad decision. Almost. She refused to lose her head to a stunning Farington landscape and a gorgeous Gainsborough.

Isabelle stepped toward the latter painting and gestured toward one of the girls in the portrait. "Is that your grandmother?"

"Yes," Val said.

She looked at him and then the painting in wonder. "Gainsborough painted your family?"

"My great-grandfather and his children, yes. My great-grandmother had already died." Val turned to the butler, who'd let them in. "Is my grandmother still out?

"Yes, Your Grace. With Lady Viola," the butler said, casting a surreptitious glance toward Isabelle.

Val gestured toward her. "Blenheim, allow me to present Mrs. Cortland. She will be Grandmama's guest for a while. Please have her luggage fetched from my coach. "

Isabelle hoped he hadn't spoken out of turn. What if the dowager refused to welcome her?

"We'll wait for Grandmama in the drawing room." Val swept his hand toward the stairs, and Isabelle preceded him. She was all too aware of her plain gray frock that until a short while ago had been covered with a barmaid's apron. And now she found herself the guest of a dowager duchess.

When they reached the drawing room, she tried not to rush around from spectacular painting to breathtaking sculpture. She turned and looked at Val. "What if she doesn't want me here?"

"I already told you that won't happen."

"Your grandmother seems to be a woman with a mind of her own." Isabelle admired that.

"She will see the benefit in this for all parties. My grandmother's mind is exceptionally sharp."

Isabelle didn't doubt it. She allowed herself a slow perusal of the room. If she was going to stay here, at least for a little while, she'd have plenty of time to explore everything. "Does your grandmother have a library like yours?" she asked, glancing back at Val, who had taken up a position near the fire leaning against the mantelpiece.

"Not as large as mine, but you'll be satisfied. Viola likes to read almost as much as she likes to write."

"She's a writer?" Isabelle hadn't known that. "What does she write?"

"I'll let her tell you about that," Val said, sounding a bit short. Was he still angry with her? Wasn't she still angry with him?

Maybe a little. Mostly she was frustrated with her situation. She'd felt lucky to have been hired as a bar-maid at a respectable establishment. It wasn't her first choice in employment, of course, but given that she hadn't been able to stay in Lord Barkley's employ, she hadn't possessed the luxury of passing it up. She'd planned to continue her search for a governess or teaching position and hoped her job at the Wicked Duke would be temporary.

The Wicked Duke... How had she not known immediately that it belonged to Val and Colehaven? They had been renowned as the wicked dukes.

She stood in front of a Grecian urn on the other side of the room from Val and stole a glance in his direction. He stared down at the hearth, his mouth twisted into a frown.

What on earth was she doing here? He'd been right—she couldn't work in his tavern, and not just because she couldn't afford to be seen there. She couldn't work in his tavern because it was *his* tavern. Because being around him only reminded her of what she'd lost. No, of what she'd never had.

And never would.

Now she found herself still in his vicinity ensconced with his grandmother and sister. She needed to find a new job fast.

"You don't have to wait with me," she said.

He looked over at her. "I don't mind."

"You should get back to the Feast of St. Valentine." In truth, she was sorry to miss the festivities. It looked to be a smashing good time. "It is your day, after all."

They'd laughed about that ten years ago. He'd given her a valentine and told her she had to accept it because it was his day. He'd made it himself and written several lines of truly abysmal poetry. She still had it, pressed between the pages of her beloved copy of *Les Liaisons dangereuses*.

She wondered if he'd given valentines to anyone else. His wife, probably. Or not, since he'd indicated it hadn't been a happy union. She left the urn and walked toward him. "Is there no one to whom you want to give a valentine?"

His gaze snapped to hers. "Are you flirting with me, Isabelle?" The question was a mix of teasing and darkness. The tone of it made her shiver and reminded her of how dangerous it was to be alone with him. Last night, she'd tested the bounds of temptation when she'd kissed him.

"No. I was simply making conversation." She turned from him and went to the corner of the room where a large landscape hung.

It was some time before he spoke. "I'm sorry you feel cornered."

She realized he sounded closer. Turning, she saw that he'd moved toward her but still stood several feet away. It felt as though they were circling each other like hunter and prey. Who was which? She refused to be the victim.

"I appreciate you saying that."

"I do think you'll be comfortable here, and it's only temporary."

"I just realized I may receive responses to inquiries at your address. I do hope you'll forward my correspondence."

"Of course." He raked his hand through his hair, freeing that familiar lock from the style so that it fell across his forehead. "I hope you realize I've only been trying to help you."

"And I hope you realize that my situation is far different from yours. I need employment. Furthermore, I like employment. I like feeling useful and providing for myself."

"You like being independent."

She clasped her hands in front of her waist and inclined her head. "Quite."

"I would say that I'm sorry your husband left you in a state where you needed to provide for yourself, but you seem content."

Oh, she'd been angry at first. He'd gambled away everything and had left her with what would have been a ruinous amount of debt if not for the money her father had left her. She'd vowed she would take care of herself and not rely upon anyone.

Commotion carried from the stairs into the drawing room.

"They must be home," Val murmured, turning toward the door.

Isabelle straightened and squeezed her hands together. It was silly to be nervous—she'd met the dowager before—but she was nonetheless. Her ire was also pricking anew because Val had just reminded her of the promise she'd made to herself— that she would rely only upon herself. She ought to take her things and go right to Prudence's. Not that she knew where that was…

It seemed she had nowhere else to go.

The dowager and Lady Viola entered the drawing room. The former peered at Isabelle with a hooded gaze while the latter came toward her with a broad smile. "Blenheim says you're staying with us. How lovely!"

The dowager sat in a dark red chair near the hearth and looked directly at her grandson. "Explain."

"Mrs. Cortland is between employment at the moment, and I've hired her to act as Viola's chaperone."

Lady Viola made a sound in her throat that was part cough and part gasp, but she said nothing.

"Viola doesn't need a chaperone," the dowager said, confirming what Isabelle had said and Val had disputed.

"This will allow you to have more freedom," Val said. "Anyway, it's a temporary situation while she secures employment. She can't very well stay with me."

"Did Lord Barkley dismiss her?" the dowager asked, causing Isabelle's breath to catch. "Never mind, I can see he did." She exhaled, and Isabelle couldn't tell if she was put out or not. "Run along, then, Eastleigh. I shall handle this."

What did that mean? Isabelle looked to Val in question, but he was still focused on the dowager.

"It will be so nice to have you here," Lady Viola said. "Has anyone shown you to your room yet?" When Isabelle shook her head, Lady Viola continued. "Then I shall have the honor."

Val clapped his hands together. "It looks as though you both have things well in hand." He bowed toward Isabelle. "I'll deliver your correspondence straightaway."

He would, or he'd send someone with it? She hoped it was the latter. It would be best if they stayed apart. The temptation to kiss him again—or worse—was too great. Even when he made her angry with his arrogance.

Then he was gone, and the dowager instantly spoke. "Sit, gel. And tell me why Lord Barkley dismissed you."

Feeling as though she were about to stand trial, Isabelle started toward the dowager. Lady Viola met her halfway and linked her arm through Isabelle's with an encouraging smile. She guided her to the settee and they sat down together. Lady Viola removed her arm and situated the gauzy lilac skirt of her ball gown so that it draped elegantly over her legs to the floor. It was the finest material Isabelle had ever seen.

All too aware that the dowager awaited her answer, Isabelle folded her hands in her lap. "Lady Barkley hired a governess to replace me. In addition to their regular studies, she will teach the girls music and needlepoint and dancing until they see a dancing master, presumably."

"Because you cannot." The dowager's lips pursed with disapproval. "Perhaps I should hire a governess for you so you can learn how to dance and embroider."

Isabelle worked to keep her tone even and not defensive. "I know how to dance." *Not well.*

"Is this new governess as educated as you are?" the dowager asked.

"No."

"Then why didn't Lord Barkley keep you on and hire this other woman in addition?"

"I wondered the same thing, Your Grace. It is my belief that Lady Barkley didn't care for my closeness with her daughters."

"Jealous?" The dowager's lip curled. "A pitiful emotion. One cannot be jealous of a child's relationship with her governess. If they are fond of her, so much the better." She eyed Isabelle for a moment as if she were searching for some defect. "Are you certain her jealousy wasn't due to another source?"

Lady Viola, who was seated closer to the dowager, leaned toward her. "Grandmama, you can't be insinuating Mrs. Cortland behaved inappropriately with Lord Barkley!"

Isabelle kept her jaw from dropping. But the dowager was correct—in a way. "She was jealous of me," Isabelle said quietly. "I think it's possible, anyway. Lord Barkley made it clear it was not his decision to replace me, and that he'd fought for me to stay."

"For less than magnanimous reasons, I'm sure." The dowager's hazel eyes flickered with malice, and Isabelle renewed her vow to never find herself on the woman's bad side. "I wondered if that were the case."

"How did you know?"

"I'm exceptionally clever, my dear. One, you are an attractive, intelligent woman, and, if memory serves, Lady Barkley is neither of those things. Second, you did not remain in their employ and now find yourself in a difficult position requiring help from quarters you would probably not normally accept."

How had the dowager determined all that, particularly the latter? "I am grateful for your assistance," Isabelle said. She was, even if she hadn't sought it.

"I'm certain you are, just as I am certain it wounds your pride to have to accept this arrangement. I sized you up within an hour of meeting you, my dear. You may stay as long as necessary, and if you would like assistance with securing a new position, you need only ask." She rose, and Lady Viola leapt up to help her.

"Do you need help getting upstairs?" Lady Viola asked.

"Not tonight, dear. My aches are much improved today, as they always are when the rain stops."

Lady Viola kissed the dowager's pale cheek. "Good night, Grandmama."

"Good night," Isabelle said, standing. "And thank you."

The dowager left, and Lady Viola turned back to face Isabelle. "I meant what I said—it's just lovely that you're here. I hope it takes you all Season to secure a new position." She winced. "My apologies. That's rather selfish of me. Unless you'd like to spend the Season with me."

Isabelle had never dreamed of having a Season, and the idea of mingling with Society's "best" didn't appeal to her in the slightest. However, spending time with Lady Viola had a certain appeal, and it had nothing to do with her being Val's sister. Lady Viola possessed a warm and magnetic nature. She was, perhaps, the first woman Isabelle could conceive of calling friend.

"I should like for you to give me a proper tour of the house tomorrow so that I may appreciate everything. Your grandmother's collection of art is magnificent."

"I should love to! But for now, I should show you to your room. Blenheim said your things were already taken there and unpacked."

It was as if she were an honored guest. She'd never been that before. "It's very kind of your grandmother to allow me to stay. Val—" Damn! His name escaped her mouth before she could stop it. She could only hope Lady Viola hadn't caught it, however, given the slight widening of her eyes, Isabelle was all but certain she had. "His Grace was adamant she would welcome me, but I didn't wish to intrude."

"You couldn't possibly. Grandmama likes you—she said as much. Honestly, she gave you high praise."

Isabelle thought back to what the dowager had said and couldn't determine what that might have been. "Hopefully it won't be for very long. I've sent several inquiries already."

"Well, I shall hope for the opposite. I've a mind that we should be friends, and if you leave too soon, I won't be able to find out why you called my brother Val." Her eyes twinkled with merriment.

Isabelle's insides curled. Just what had she gotten herself into?

CHAPTER 10

*I*sabelle's chamber at the dowager's house boasted a variety of paintings as awe inducing as the ones she'd seen the night before. It was as if she were staying at Somerset House. Not that she'd ever been to Somerset House, but she could imagine the same kinds of paintings were on display there, simply in greater quantity.

She'd slept well in a bed dressed with silken sheets and adorned with velvet hangings. Indeed, she felt rather decadent.

The dowager apparently broke her fast in her chamber, but Isabelle was delighted to join Lady Viola in the morning room, which had a wall of tall windows and glass doors that looked out to the enclosed garden. Shortly after they were seated, Lady Viola insisted Isabelle call her simply Viola. She'd said they were now friends, after all.

"What shall we do today?" Viola asked once she'd finished her toast and eggs. "I recall you saying on our shopping trip that this was your first time in London. You must have a list of things you'd like to see and do."

"Not a formal list, no. I'd like to see the British

Museum. And Somerset House. And maybe Hatchards."

"Did I hear someone say Hatchards?" Val stepped into the morning room and extended his leg before joining them at the table. He looked to Isabelle. "As it happens, I came to take you to Hatchards."

"And me, I hope," Viola said. "Mrs. Cortland is *my* chaperone, if you recall."

Val rolled his eyes. "Yes, you may come too."

"How generous of you to offer," she said sweetly. "Next time you make plans for *my* chaperone, you should make sure we don't have other engagements."

Isabelle suppressed a smile at their mock bickering. At least it didn't seem genuine. It was lively and amusing and rather endearing.

"*Do* you have other plans?" he asked, looking between his sister and Isabelle.

"No," Isabelle answered.

"The point was we might've," Viola said, standing. "And you're in luck because Hatchards was on our list. Shall we go?"

Val inclined his head. "Indeed. First, however, I thought Mrs. Cortland might like to visit Dangerfield's across the square."

Viola studied him intently, then transferred her gaze to Isabelle. The curiosity in her stare made Isabelle shift uncomfortably. She got to her feet. "You remembered that I said I liked to visit circulating libraries," she said, hoping that might provide sufficient explanation to Viola as to why Val might know that about her.

"I did."

"We'll just fetch our things," Viola said, her gaze still lingering on her brother and Isabelle.

She left the morning room first, and as Isabelle followed, she considered how to caution Val. If they weren't careful, Viola—or worse, his grandmother—would deduce the depth of their acquaintance.

A short while later, they walked into the circulating library. Viola went straight to the section of new acquisitions, while Isabelle meandered in the opposite direction. As she perused a book of poetry, Val approached her with another gentleman.

"Mr. Dangerfield, allow me to present Mrs. Cortland. Mrs. Cortland, this is Mr. Dangerfield, the proprietor of this circulating library."

Isabelle dipped a curtsey. "Pleased to meet you, Mr. Dangerfield. You have a wonderful collection."

"Thank you. I understand your father was warden at Merton College. I attended Wadham, though I heard your father speak on occasion." The man's dark gaze softened. "I was sorry to hear he'd passed."

She inclined her head. "I appreciate your kindness."

Val clasped his hands behind his back. "Mr. Dangerfield is in need of assistance with his library, and I've recommended you for the position."

Isabelle blinked at him, completely surprised at this revelation. She looked at Mr. Dangerfield. "You'd like me to work here?"

"I have been looking for someone to help me decide what to acquire for the library as well as work here a few days each week. If you would be interested, I'd be delighted to have you."

Interested? It was perfect. And Val had made it happen. She glanced toward him as warm gratitude spread through her chest. "I would be honored, thank you."

Mr. Dangerfield grinned broadly. "Excellent."

They made arrangements for her to return on Monday morning, and Mr. Dangerfield left them. Isabelle turned to Val. "How did you know he was looking for someone?"

"I can see how important your independence is, and how much you hate the corner you've been backed into. I thought you might enjoy working in a bookshop or a library. I took a chance and stopped in here this morning and was fortunate that Mr. Dangerfield was, in fact, in search of help."

"It's almost too good to be true," she said softly.

"I have thought that many times about you."

His words made her heart flutter, but she refused to bask in that sensation. "You must be careful. I think your sister suspects something." Isabelle glanced toward Viola, who was thumbing through a book on the other side of the library.

His gaze followed hers. "Why would you think that?"

Isabelle winced. "I may have inadvertently referred to you by your Christian name."

His attention shifted back to her, his eyes widening briefly. "And she caught it?"

"Most definitely. Then you arrived this morning and suggested I might like to visit a circulating library, possibly giving the impression we are more than recent acquaintances. It's questionable enough that you've taken it upon yourself to help me to the point of lodging me with your grandmother."

He exhaled. "I see your point. I will do my best to leave you alone."

Isabelle saw Viola replace her book on the shelf and turn toward them. "She's coming," Isabelle whispered. She affixed a smile to her lips. "The most extraordinary thing has just happened. Mr. Dangerfield offered me a position working here."

Viola blinked in surprise. "That *is* extraordinary. Would you have wanted to do that?"

"In fact, I *am* going to do that. It's an excellent solution, at least for the short term." The pay

wouldn't be enough to sustain her, but it would ensure she had her own funds without stealing from
her savings. She needed that to start her school.

"I'm not sure Grandmama will approve," Viola
said gently.

"I'll handle Grandmama," Val said, and Isabelle
shot him a warning glance. He couldn't keep inter-
vening on her behalf. It was beyond suspicious, and
Viola was far too clever not to notice. She'd *already*
noticed.

"If she'd rather I didn't stay, I will understand,"
Isabelle interjected. "Your Grace, you needn't speak
with her. If you please." She hoped he understood
what she was trying to convey.

"Of course you'll stay," Viola declared. "*I* will
handle Grandmama. You are *my* chaperone, after all,
and I've decided I need you."

They departed Dangerfield's and went to
Hatchards, where Isabelle immersed herself in the
splendor of books and the environment of people
who loved books. She could happily have lived there.

Val stayed away from her, as he said he would. It
was best for everyone if they ignored the past—both
the distant and recent—and focused on a future in
which their lives did not intersect. After she left his
grandmother's. For now, they were at least in each
other's orbit. Hopefully he would not come round
and take her to libraries or bookshops anymore.

And how that depressed her. That he'd thought
to inquire after a position for her was incredibly
touching. It seemed he did understand her. Perhaps
as no one ever had.

Her husband certainly hadn't bothered. He'd spent
all his time gambling, except for when he rode his horse
or walked with his dogs—anything to spend time away
from her. When she hadn't swelled with child in three

years of marriage, he'd stopped coming to her bed, not that she'd minded. He'd been a cursory bedmate, which was better than what he might have been, but so much worse than what she'd hoped. Val had set her up for certain disappointment. She'd known she would always compare her husband to him, but when the former had turned out to be so lacking, it was impossible not to agonize over what she was missing.

And what Val's wife had possessed.

The dowager's words came back to her—jealousy was a pitiful emotion. She was right, and Isabelle had worked very hard not to dwell in it.

When they returned to Berkeley Square, Val accompanied them inside. Deciding it was best if she spent as little time with him as possible, even in the company of others, Isabelle escaped to her room. There, she wrote more letters to schools that might be hiring, as far away as York. Distance would ease the ache of loss.

It would also put an end to temptation.

~

*V*al accompanied his sister and Isabelle into the house. Even though Viola had said she would deal with their grandmother regarding Isabelle's new job, and he should probably keep his nose out of Isabelle's affairs, he wanted to ensure Viola was able to manage the situation.

After this, he would step away. He'd done all he could. He'd made sure Isabelle was safely lodged and had a job, which was most important to her. There was nothing more he could do. Rather, there was nothing more she would allow.

Grandmama greeted them in the library, which was just off the entrance hall. "Eastleigh, don't you have better things to do than squire Viola and her chaperone about?"

"It was my pleasure to do so," he said smoothly.

Viola took a chair near the dowager. "He helped Mrs. Cortland secure a position at Dangerfield's." She looked up at him, almost daring him to dispute her.

She knew he had orchestrated it? Hell, she must have overheard their conversation with Dangerfield? She must have. Val had thought they were far enough away across the shop. He worked very hard not to scowl at his sister.

Grandmama stared at him expectantly. "Is that so?"

"She is looking for employment, and I was merely trying to help her."

"Are you aware of why she left Barkley's employ prematurely?" Grandmama asked.

Of course he knew. She'd found a job—at his tavern. But he wasn't going to tell his grandmother that. "It wasn't really premature," Val said. "Barkley dismissed her."

"Don't you find her dismissal strange?" Grandmama mused. "She's incredibly qualified and capable at what she does. Any intelligent person would simply have hired a second governess to teach what she doesn't. However, Barkley didn't do that. Barkley terminated her employment."

What the devil was she getting at? "Grandmama, I've never known you not to speak plainly."

"And I've never known you to be obtuse. The blackguard had a tendre for Mrs. Cortland, and Lady Barkley knew it. Hence, Lady Barkley got rid of her."

Fury squeezed at Val's insides, and it was all he could do not to go home and throw Barkley out. No, he'd punch him first, and *then* he'd throw him out.

And maybe punch him again. "She didn't tell me that."

"And why should she? You were simply her host, barely an acquaintance. Yet here you are managing her affairs—securing her lodgings and finding her employment. Good heavens, Eastleigh, if you want to make her your mistress, do so already." Grandmama turned her head briefly toward Viola. "Pretend you didn't hear that, dear."

Viola blew out a breath. "I'm five and twenty, Grandmama. I am not unaware of the world."

"I'd prefer to think you are unaware of such arrangements, even if you are not," she said crisply. "Humor me."

"I do not wish to make her my mistress," Val said through somewhat gritted teeth. He wasn't lying exactly. He hadn't thought to make her his mistress—she would never agree. But now that it had been suggested…

No.

"Then, let her alone." Grandmama's tone was stern as she narrowed her eyes up at him. "If you spent half this much time in the pursuit of a wife, you might actually find one."

Val had endured enough on that subject. If only his grandmother knew how much he did, in fact, humor her. "I am not ready to take another wife, and I'd appreciate it very much if you'd stop pressing the matter."

Grandmama's eyes blazed with irritation. "What on earth are you waiting for? I understand your reticence, but it's been three years. You will not make the same mistake twice." She stood. "I will look after Mrs. Cortland, and in exchange, you will join me at Almack's next week. I promise it won't be painful."

She departed the library, leaving Val to stare after

her in anger and disbelief. "The hell it won't be," he muttered.

"I'm sorry about that," Viola said quietly, reminding him of her presence since he'd quite forgotten she was even there. "But you invited it upon yourself."

He jerked his head toward his annoying sibling. "And what should I have done, let Mrs. Cortland fend for herself?" Because that was what would have happened. She wasn't going to stay in Barkley's employ, of that he was now certain. Val could hardly wait to get home and toss him out. He looked forward to having his household back to normal, and it had nothing to do with their daughters but everything to do with Lady Barkley. She was an aggravating presence.

"You might have," Viola answered. "I'm confident in Mrs. Cortland's abilities. Perhaps you should be too. I have to assume you know her better than I do."

He narrowed his eyes at her. "Assume nothing."

Viola rose, smoothing her pale blue skirts as she approached him. Touching his arm gently, she said, "I should like to be here for you, if you need me." She withdrew her hand and left.

Val surrendered to his familiar defense: he didn't need anyone.

CHAPTER 11

*T*hough she'd only started a few hours ago, Isabelle loved working at the circulating library. When she wasn't reading, she was recommending reading. She was already thinking how she might use her savings to found her own circulating library. If only books weren't so expensive. It was a crime, really. Only the wealthy could afford to buy them, and even circulating libraries weren't free. Plus, you had to return the books, which in some cases had caused Isabelle great heartache.

Isabelle looked up from her book as the shop door opened. Then she gasped in delighted surprise as Beatrice and Caroline dashed toward her.

She'd barely stood from the stool before both girls had wrapped their arms around her. She held them close, basking in their warmth and their familiar sweet scents. Looking toward the door, she braced herself, assuming she would see the new governess or Lady Barkley.

She only saw Val.

"You brought them?" she asked.

The girls stepped back from her but didn't let her go—Beatrice clutched her left hand while Caroline clasped her right.

"He said he had a surprise," Caroline said, grinning. "It's a wonderful one, isn't it?"

"The very best." Isabelle laughed. "Now, tell me what I have missed."

Caroline launched into a diatribe detailing the horrors of needlepoint and the dangers of dancing, then Beatrice complained about Miss Shipley's terrible pronunciation of French.

"She's atrocious," Beatrice lamented. "Your ears would bleed."

Isabelle stifled another laugh as she glanced toward Val. Only he wasn't there. Where had he gone?

Caroline sighed. "I never thought I'd say this, but I miss Greek."

"Miss Shipley doesn't teach it at all?" Isabelle asked.

Both girls shook their heads. "And Mama doesn't care." Beatrice's tone was derisive. "I've been keeping up with it, however. As well as I can. His Grace helped me with some this morning, actually. That's when he said he had a surprise for us."

Val was helping them with Greek in addition to bringing them to see her? First he'd found her a job and now he was filling the hole in her heart that had formed when she'd had to leave her charges. Was he simply trying to make up for his authoritarian behavior when he'd dismissed her from the tavern?

Or was it something more?

She wasn't sure she dared contemplate the latter.

"How wonderful that His Grace is helping you," Isabelle said.

Beatrice looked down at the floor for a moment. "Well, that can't last since we're moving to Queen Street tomorrow."

Isabelle's chest ached at the melancholy in Beatrice's tone. She wished things could be different, but there was nothing any of them could do.

Squeezing their hands, Isabelle sank down so she was more on eye level with Caroline and had to look up a bit at Beatrice. "Change can be difficult but also wonderful. Perhaps you will fall in love with playing the pianoforte."

"Mama is making us learn guitar." Caroline stuck out her tongue.

"You may enjoy it. The point is to keep an open mind. If you don't, you might miss the wonders that life has to offer. And I do hope you will give Miss Shipley a fair chance. She is not me, and she shouldn't try to be."

"But we want you," Caroline whined.

Beatrice nodded in agreement. "We miss you."

"I miss you too." Isabelle's throat tightened, but she refused to let them see her emotions. "I shall write to you often, and you must write back to me."

Caroline scowled. "What if Mama won't let us?"

Had the baroness said that? A wave of anger swept over Isabelle, and she again worked to keep a positive tone and a kind expression. "I'm sure she will."

"I'll strongly suggest she does."

Isabelle jerked her head up and saw Val standing just a few feet away. Where had he come from?

Beatrice gave him a tentative smile. "Thank you, Your Grace."

"It's my pleasure. You girls better choose the books you want, or we won't have an excuse for our outing." He winked at them, and they looked toward Isabelle.

"Will you help us choose?" Caroline said.

"Of course. You may have two each." She met Val's gaze. "On your membership?"

He inclined his head. "If you please."

Oh, she pleased. She was so overwhelmed by his kindness and thoughtfulness, she could kiss him.

Or maybe she just wanted to kiss him because he was Val. And the Val of today seemed to be every bit the Val she remembered, only better.

She helped the girls select their books, and in all too short a time, they were on their way. Now that they knew she was here, they promised to visit as much as they could. With a final hug, she waved them off, then hurried back to the counter, where she dashed away her tears.

Later that afternoon, she returned to Berkeley Square feeling satisfied after her first day at the library, as well as a lingering sadness over missing the girls.

"Isabelle?" Viola called her by her first name now since she'd asked Isabelle to call her Viola. "Come into the library!"

Isabelle turned right into the library, where Viola was bent over a table. She had a map of the world spread out before her and didn't look up as Isabelle walked in.

"How was the library?" Viola asked as she picked up a pencil and scratched a note on a piece of parchment set atop the map.

"Wonderful, thank you. I think I may have found my passion."

Viola straightened and turned her head to Isabelle. "I thought teaching was your passion?"

"It is. It was." Isabelle loved teaching, but the life of a governess was rather solitary and, as a result, lonely. She'd developed a close relationship with the girls, but now that was gone and she had no one. The thought of starting over with a new family was less than appealing. "I enjoy the bustle of the library."

"That's marvelous," Viola said. "Perhaps it's a blessing that your last position...ended." She shook

her head. "I had to pause and think of how to describe that."

Ended seemed as good a description as any. "The
girls came to the library today." Isabelle didn't mention that Val had brought them. Viola didn't need
any more evidence that their association was more
than they'd let on.

Viola leaned her hip against the table and stuck
her pencil into her upswept blonde hair. "Was it nice
to see them, or is it difficult since their parents are so
horrid?"

"It was very nice. I would never blame them for
their parents' failings. Indeed, I wouldn't want them
to know about their parents. They have time enough
to learn for themselves, though I suppose I hope they
never do, particularly when it comes to their father."
Isabelle shuddered.

Viola's nostrils flared. "He didn't...do anything
untoward, did he? I mean, physically."

"If you're asking whether he attacked me, no. He
touched me in a way he hadn't before, and thankfully, I was able to walk away without provoking
him." She felt grateful when she thought of how
much worse it could have been.

Viola snorted. "Men are terrible. Most men, anyway. I do like my brother, but in my mind, he isn't a
man. He's my brother."

In Isabelle's mind, he was most definitely a man
and was definitely *not* disgusting. Her husband, on
the other hand... "I can't disagree with you."

"Of course, women can be just as bad," Viola
mused. "Take Val's wife. She was awful."

She shouldn't ask, but Viola couldn't help herself.
"How was she awful?"

"She was reckless and indiscreet, always staying
out until all hours gambling and generally behaving

as a wanton instead of a duchess. She nearly sent poor Grandmama into apoplexy."

Isabelle had no idea, and why should she have? It was no wonder Val had been unhappy. "What happened to her?" Again, she shouldn't ask, but was utterly unable to remain silent.

"She was with child and lost the babe. She didn't survive either." Viola looked down, her brow creasing. "Grandmama said it was for the best. I say 'poor Grandmama,' but it was Val who bore the brunt of Louisa's behavior."

Had he loved her? Had she broken his heart? These were more questions Isabelle longed to ask but decided she couldn't. None of this was her business, and she was ignoring her own warnings about not showing the depth of her relationship with Val to his family.

However he'd felt toward his wife, Isabelle ached for him. Losing a child was worse than not being able to have them. At least that was what she, as someone who apparently couldn't have one, surmised.

Viola looked at her with a sly, secretive smile. "I think I should take you out tonight."

"I couldn't," Isabelle protested. "I haven't a thing to wear." Never mind the fact that she didn't want to.

"I have clothes you can borrow, and this isn't a Society event. I want to take you where I go sometimes. It's devilish fun, and you can be completely anonymous. Are you up for it?"

Anonymous? In London? And it wasn't Society?

A slow grin lifted Isabelle's lips. "What time shall we leave?"

～

"$\mathcal{T}$arleton!"

Val didn't look up from his tankard at the chorus that rose upon the entry of his friend Hugh Tarleton. He was too intent on brooding.

Hugh sat down beside him. "Eastleigh, are you drunk?"

"Not yet."

"He's been like that all evening," Jack said. "Maybe you can deliver him an uplifting sermon."

"If you want to hear a sermon, come to church." Hugh's deep, commanding voice rumbled over the table.

Jack chuckled. "Not your church. I'd like to keep the contents of my pockets intact, thank you."

Hugh was rector at St. Giles in the Fields, in the very center of some of London's worst neighborhoods. "Your pockets would be fine. No one dares steal at my church."

Val didn't doubt it. Hugh was a mammoth of a man with massive shoulders and arms that looked as though they could break you in two.

"Why are you getting drunk?" Hugh asked as one of the barmaids deposited his mug before him.

"Seems like a good idea." Because then he could forget about Isabelle, at least for a short time. He had to stop torturing himself as he'd done today when he'd taken Barkley's girls to the library. He'd done it because the poor things had been so forlorn since Isabelle had left, and Val felt sorry for them having such terrible parents. But if he were honest with himself, he'd also done it to see Isabelle.

Not just see her—he'd done it to please her. And judging from her reaction, he'd done that. The problem was, having done that, he wanted to keep doing it. And the problem with *that* was the fact that he had no occasion to do so. She was not his to please.

He finished the ale in front of him and signaled for a refill.

The door opened, but there was no chorus. This happened from time to time as not everyone who came in was a regular patron. They likely soon would be, however, so it was not surprising when someone immediately welcomed the newcomer. *Newcomers.*

Val glanced up and saw two young gentlemen. They were both rather thin, and they both sported far too much facial hair. Val assumed they'd had the pox, and their beards covered the scars.

"Would you care to sit with us?" Hugh invited.

"No, thank you," one answered. "We're for the billiards room. Er, do you have a billiards room? We heard you might."

Val narrowed his eyes at the shorter of the two who'd spoken. There was something about that voice…

"We do, in fact," Jack answered. "I'd be happy to show you." He stood and went to the bar. "Doyle, a pair of ales for these fine gentlemen."

"Already poured." Doyle slid them across the bar with a smile. "Welcome to the Wicked Duke, lads."

The shorter man picked up his mug, then shot a look at the other man when he hesitated. There was something very odd about them. Val slowly rose. "I'll come along with you, if you don't mind."

"Of course they don't mind," Jack said. "They wouldn't turn the owner away." He stage-whispered to the two gentlemen, "This is the Duke of Eastleigh, one of the 'Wicked Dukes' the place is named for. He generally gets what he wants." Jack winked at him, and Val rolled his eyes. He also noted that the taller of the two gentlemen looked straight at him and then quickly averted his gaze as if meeting Val's eyes could set him on fire.

Val asked Doyle for the key to the ball box and followed the gentlemen, who were led by Jack, into the billiard room. It adjoined both the main and private parlors, but the doors were kept closed since the lighting in the billiard room was far brighter than anywhere else in the pub.

One of the four tables was already in use, as a pair of gentlemen were at play beneath the oil lamps. They warmly welcomed Jack and Val and the new arrivals.

"Here you are," Jack said. "Have you played before?"

The tall gentleman shook his head, while the shorter one nodded. "Many times."

Val went to the locked box where they kept the valuable ivory balls, and withdrew a set. He set the two white cue balls and the red ball on the nearest table and relocked the box.

Jack inclined his head toward the taller gentleman. "Good luck to you." Then he turned to Val. "I'm going back to the salon. You coming?"

Val was far too interested in uncovering the mystery of these two gentlemen. He had his suspicions and felt certain he could confirm them in relatively short order. "No, I'm going to stay and watch."

The taller gentleman shot a look toward Val, and it was all he needed. He knew those cobalt eyes, and they didn't belong to a man. He also knew the voice of the other man because he, rather *she*, came in here often, though in a different disguise. Clearly, Viola was trying to mask her identity because if Val knew it was her, he'd likely recognize her friend. Which begged the question, why would Viola risk it? Surely she would know he'd puzzle it out.

The perimeter of the room contained a handful

of tables and chairs for spectators. Val situated himself in a chair nearest their billiard table and settled in to be entertained. "How many points will you play to?" he asked.

"Six," Viola answered as she moved to the wall and selected a cue rather than a mace. What would Isabelle choose? Did she even know the difference?

Suddenly, Val couldn't resist the opportunity before him. He stood and joined her at the wall. "Since this is your first time, may I recommend a cue? They are far more accurate than the mace." He selected one and offered it to her, noting that she kept her gaze from meeting his. "The leather on the end will help guide the ball as you seek to strike the others on the table or if you can achieve a hazard point."

"A hazard point is when you put one of the other balls in a pocket," Viola said, careful to keep her voice pitched low. Viola explained the rest of the rules they would follow that night, using everything Val had taught her. If he hadn't discerned her identity before, he would have now.

"Why don't you have a few practice rounds to show your friend, Mr.—?" Val suggested.

Viola responded. "I am Mr. Gates, and this is Mr. Beaufort. I'll go first to demonstrate." She explained to Isabelle how to strategize what to hit and where, as well as showed her how to hold the cue. Viola was quite accomplished at billiards and achieved a hazard, sending the red ball into a pocket.

"That doesn't look terribly difficult."

Val bit his lip lest he laugh at the comically low pitch of Isabelle's voice. "Go on and give it a try."

Isabelle assessed the table and went up to the edge. She realized she was too close and took a step back. Then she angled her cue and missed hitting the ball entirely.

Viola sniggered, and Isabelle shot her a heated look. Val swallowed a laugh. "May I show you?"

He took a cue from the wall and moved to her side of the table to model how she should approach the shot. "You want to hold the cue so that you can control its movement. Like this." He gripped it low and then guided the upper portion with his other hand.

She tried to mimic what he did, but still wasn't quite mastering the stance or grip. He leaned his cue against the table and stepped behind her to position her arms.

That was a mistake.

She may have been dressed like a man, but he was all too aware she was a woman. And not just any woman, but Isabelle, the source of every dream he'd ever had.

He tried to keep the contact minimal, but it didn't matter. At this proximity, her scent filled his senses. Moving quickly, he adjusted her grip on the lower part of the cue, then reached around and leaned forward, his chest pressing against her back as he showed her how to guide the stick toward the ball. Then he demonstrated, controlling her movements.

The cue struck her ball and hit Viola's. And Val tore himself away before he was unable to.

He picked up the cue and replaced it on the wall. "Very nice." He meant it to describe her strike, but it applied to so much more.

Oh, this was madness.

He went back to his chair and the table where he'd set his tankard. Lifting the mug, he took a long drink.

"More practice, I think," Viola said. "You go again."

Isabelle bent and took aim, and Val swore he saw

her tremble. Madness didn't begin to describe it. Because he should go. Instead, he sat there and watched her practice several shots.

A small group—five gentlemen—came into the room, their laughter filling the space. "Glad there's a table free," one said.

"Two, actually," Viola said cheerily. "But there's five of you. Who's not playing?"

"We'll take turns," one said.

Val rose and went to unlock the ball box. They took two sets and set up the remaining two tables. Soon the billiard room was alive with boisterous conversation and good-natured wagering.

"Are you ready to start the game?" Viola asked Isabelle.

"As ready as I will be."

At Isabelle's insistence, Viola went first, scoring a point when she hit Isabelle's cue ball. Isabelle then hit her ball, but it barely moved. She grunted in frustration as Viola moved to take another shot.

She missed, and it was the start of two missed shots by both of them. On her third try, Isabelle hit the ball so hard, it skipped over the rail and hit one of the gentlemen at the next table in the back.

"Oh!" She slapped her hand to her mouth, and it was such a ladylike gasp and action that Val jumped to his feet.

He swept up Isabelle's ale and handed her the tankard. "Don't know your own strength there, Beaufort."

Her gaze barely met his before she buried it in her mug and took a long drink, draining the vessel.

"Looks like you're in need of more ale," Val said. "Allow me to show you the brewery, and you can try a few samples." It was time for her to go before she completely exposed her disguise. He turned to Viola.

"Would you like to come along?" It wasn't supposed to be a question.

Viola, however, thought it was. "No, thank you. I've still some beer left. I'm sure one of these other gentlemen will be happy to shoot in Beaufort's place."

"I will!" This came from the odd man who wasn't currently engaged in one of the other games. Val knew him, of course, just as he knew everyone else in the room. It didn't trouble him to leave Viola here alone with them. She came to the tavern dressed as a man—the jolly Tavistock—on occasion so that she could pen her column for *The Lady's Gazette*, "Observations on Gentlemen."

Val couldn't tell if Viola was aware he knew their identity but decided it didn't matter just then. He'd tell Isabelle to be more discreet or she'd have to leave. If she chose the latter, he'd come back and inform "Gates" that his friend was ill and needed to depart.

Touching Isabelle's arm, Val said, "Follow me."

She hesitated, and he feared she wasn't going to come. Then she gripped her tankard and trailed him from the billiard room.

He led her through the private salon, then into the kitchen and on to the brewery. As soon as they were inside, he closed the door.

She moved into the center of the room, her back to him.

"What the devil are you doing here?" he asked.

She half turned, her head pitched down, and her voice dropped to that ridiculous level that was amusing and yet somehow also carried a dark sensuality. "I beg your pardon?"

Val strode forward, intent on exposing her scheme. He wasn't entirely sure how until he reached her, and then it was obvious. He pulled her into his arms and kissed her.

The hair of her beard tickled his face, and he might have laughed at the absurdity of it if he hadn't been instantly swept away by the touch of her tongue as she opened her mouth in surprise.

Cupping the back of her neck, Val dislodged her hat and plunged his fingers into her hair. Pins went flying, and the silken locks splashed over his hand as his mouth danced with hers.

She pulled back, her hand moving to the back of her head and connecting with his. "You've ruined my costume!"

"Your costume wasn't very convincing. Or do you think I go around kissing strange gentlemen?" He was torn between laughter and overwhelming desire. Despite the hair covering the lower half of her face and her masculine attire, he'd never wanted her more.

She dropped her hand to her side. "I'm sure I don't know. Mayhap you like the feel of a beard."

"I think I might, at least in this instance. Shall I try again to make certain, or would you prefer to take it off?"

She looked about, then sauntered to a worktable where she set her empty tankard down. Then she faced him, her gaze sultry, and her lips parted in provocative invitation. "I think I'll take it off. Tell me, Your Grace, does that door lock?"

CHAPTER 12

*I*sabelle should not have asked such a thing, and yet she couldn't bring herself to take it back. Already stimulated by this daring escapade with Viola and the tankard of beer she'd consumed, it hadn't taken much for her attraction toward Val to rise to a dangerous level. When he'd helped her to position the cue, her entire body had come alive, both in memory and in anticipation. She wanted to know if being with him would feel as good now as it had ten years ago.

There was only one way she was going to find out.

Val stared at her, his eyes narrowing slightly and his nostrils flaring. The muscle in his jaw grew taut, and then he suddenly spun around. He didn't move, however; he simply stood there for a moment. Then he sprang into action and dragged a barrel in front of the door.

It wasn't a lock, but she supposed it would do. Lifting her hand to her face, she gently pulled at the beard, which Viola had applied with a paste she'd insisted was safe, that actors used it on the stage. But now, as Isabelle tried to remove the hair, she began to think it would rip her skin right off.

Joining her at the table, Val took her hand and pressed a kiss to her wrist. He then took over, carefully pulling the hair away from her face. He worked slowly, and she closed her eyes as he freed her flesh. When he was done, she heard him move and opened her eyes.

He returned with a damp cloth, which he smoothed over her cheek. Then he kissed her there, his lips caressing her with the same care as he'd taken with removing the fake beard. He moved to her other cheek and repeated the ministration. She closed her eyes again and surrendered to his touch. He wiped the cloth across her chin and kissed her there, his mouth lingering for a moment. Then the cloth stroked her lips, and her heart beat in anticipation of what would come next.

The cloth disappeared and was replaced by his lips. But this wasn't a gentle caress. This was an urgent request, a plea for her surrender.

Isabelle clasped his neck and pressed her hands against his heated flesh, opening her mouth to him and answering his entreaty with her own. The barriers of time and propriety fell away as their lips and tongues moved together.

He kissed her hard, then soft, then angled his head in a new direction, then drew back to nip at her lip. She dug her fingers into him, sliding her hands beneath his cravat—or at least trying to. Frustrated, she tugged at the silk, loosening it until the knot came free. Then she pushed her hands inside his shirt and this time had total access to his neck and collarbones. He was heat and corded muscle and divine sensation, groaning into her mouth as she explored him.

He pulled at his coat, and she helped him shrug it to the floor. She unbuttoned his waistcoat, eager to feel him against her. But wait. How were they to do this? There was no bed. No place of comfort. There was only brewing equipment.

She pulled her mouth from his and sucked in air. "Perhaps—"

He kissed her again, hard and fast, then he leaned his forehead against hers. "If you tell me we should stop, I might die. I mean, I *will* stop, but it's possible I will actually perish."

"I wasn't going to tell you to stop. I was merely going to ask if we should wait to do this until we're in a more appropriate location."

He cupped the side of her face and drew back to look into her eyes. "I don't need a bed. Or anything else. I only need you."

"I shall trust you, as I always have."

He kissed her once more, his lips searing hers with an intensity that made her knees almost buckle. She clutched at his shoulders, and he rotated her until she felt the table against her backside.

Pulling back, he untied her cravat and surveyed her costume. "While I enjoy looking at your legs encased in breeches, this would be far easier if you had worn a skirt."

She could see that now and giggled. "I hadn't planned to be seduced."

He arched a brow at her as he tossed her cravat aside and then followed it with her coat. "You're being seduced? I believe it was you who suggested I lock the door. I think I am clearly the object of the seduction."

She finished unbuttoning his waistcoat as he did the same for her. After dropping hers to the floor, he lifted her shirt over her head, leaving her upper half covered only by the length of muslin Viola had wrapped around her breasts.

He stared at it, his expression a mixture of disappointment and confusion. She pulled the end free, which was tucked between her breasts. "Unwrap," she said simply.

Taking the muslin from her fingers, he slowly unwound the fabric, his eyes meeting and holding hers. The simple task became a sensual endeavor as she was more and more liberated by the loosening of the muslin. And then it was gone, and his gaze dropped.

The sound of his indrawn breath cloaked her in heat and need, making her body pulse with desire. He reached for her, his hand lightly stroking her breast before he dragged his thumb across her nipple. She felt it harden at the precise moment she saw his eyes narrow with lust.

He bent and put his mouth on her there, his lips teasing, his tongue taunting. He tortured her for a long minute, and she closed her eyes, basking in the sensation even while she was desperate for more. She cupped his head and tugged at his hair, urging him to take more of her, to give more of himself.

And he did.

His mouth closed over her, and he sucked, sending a fierce spasm of want straight to her core. Yes, a skirt would have been far better. She could have pulled it up that very instant and urged him to come inside her.

She pressed her fingers into his scalp. "*Val.*"

He paused and looked up at her.

"I want you. Just as I did ten years ago. No, I want you more. And I know I shouldn't, that *we* shouldn't, just as I knew it then. I am helpless when it comes to you."

"Shhh." He smiled softly before he kissed her. "Not helpless," he whispered against her lips before he pulled back and stared into her eyes. "You're a woman who knows what she wants and takes it. Cole and I opened the Wicked Duke so that people could be precisely who they wanted, without pretense, without judgment, without regret."

"You have always allowed me to be exactly who I am. Except a barmaid," she teased.

"If you really want to be a barmaid, you can be a barmaid."

"I rather like being a librarian. Thank you." She pressed her lips to his. "For making that happen. For bringing me the girls today. For this."

His mouth curved into a seductive smile. "I haven't done anything yet."

"Not true, but I do want you to finish."

"Are you certain?" he asked gently, his brow creasing.

She found the hem of his shirt and swept the garment up over his chest. He helped her take it the rest of the way off, and while he was busy casting it aside, she kissed the hollow of his throat. She put her hands on his fall and began to unfasten the buttons. He palmed her nape and moaned softly as she reached into his breeches and stroked his cock.

His hips pressed forward and then he was a flurry of movement. He unbuttoned her breeches, which were thankfully far looser fitting than his, otherwise they would have been a terrible disguise, and pulled them down past her hips, then lifted her onto the table. She gasped at the sensation of the cool wood against her bare backside. Stripping her boots away, he discarded the breeches next and didn't bother with her stockings.

Need pulsed in her sex. "Touch me, Val."

He moved between her legs, claiming her mouth as he stroked his hand along her thigh. His fingers pressed into her curls, finding her clitoris, that sweet spot he'd introduced her to so long ago. The spot her husband had never even looked for. The spot she had touched so many times and thought of Val.

Never in her dreams had she imagined she'd feel him again.

Pleasure curled through her, and she ached to have him inside her. She wriggled to the edge of the table, seeking more of him. He slid his finger into her sheath, and she cried out. He kissed her, taking her exultation into himself.

Isabelle squeezed her eyes closed and completely surrendered to his sweet torment. To feel him and smell him and taste him. It was almost too much. She was going to lose herself completely, and she wasn't at all sure she wanted to be found again.

He stroked slowly at first, his thumb teasing her while he pumped his finger in and out. She moved with him, eager to reach that promised pinnacle where light met dark and the end met the beginning again. He began to move faster, touching her in precisely the way she needed to be touched. It was as if he recalled every caress, every sensation, and was recreating them exactly.

But then there were two fingers, and it was suddenly different. More. Faster. Frantic. He tore his mouth from hers and whispered against her ear, "Come for me, Isabelle."

Everything inside her split apart. She plummeted into the glorious darkness and embraced the end, knowing it was only temporary and eager for the ecstasy to begin anew.

He pulled away from her sex, and she reached between them to liberate his shaft from his clothing. He groaned while she stroked his velvety softness, the memory of it paling now that she had the reality in her grasp.

His hand covered hers, and together, they guided him to her sex. Her flesh was sensitive, and the pleasure she'd craved washed over her with stark intensity, making her gasp. She clutched his hip and pulled him into her. Obliging, he drove deep, filling her with wild abandon.

She wrapped her legs around his waist, and he scooped her against him. He kissed her, open-mouthed, his tongue dragging along hers. She felt greedy and desperate, as if she'd never have enough of him, and she supposed she wouldn't. She didn't want to think about that now. Now, she wanted to glory in this moment, in this rapture.

Their bodies moved together as if it hadn't been ten years but ten minutes since they were one. She held him tight, anchoring herself to his strength as pleasure buoyed her on a tide of passion. He moved faster, and she met him stroke for stroke as she built toward the peak once more.

Then she was there, taken completely by surprise as she descended into bliss. He was a moment behind her, filling her again and again until his muscles went taut.

She felt him start to pull away, but she held him close. "Don't go."

He cried out as his body shuddered. She smoothed her fingertips along his shoulders, his spine, taking deep breaths to return to earth.

His lips pressed against her cheek, her temple, her forehead. "I should have left your body."

"I was married for four years without issue. There is likely no need to be concerned." Likely. She supposed there was a small need, but she refused to consider it. This night was something she'd cherish for all time.

His lips claimed hers, kissing her with sweet satisfaction. She held him tight, never wanting to let go, but knowing she must. And soon.

A chill raced across her shoulders, and she shivered.

"You're cold," he murmured. Leaving her, he collected her clothing and began to help her dress. He'd tucked himself back into his breeches and rebuttoned the fall but remained shirtless. She couldn't help but appreciate the expanse of his chest and the faint curls of blond hair scattering the landscape between his nipples.

He held up the length of muslin Viola had used to wrap Isabelle's breasts. "Do we need to bind you again?"

She touched her bare face. "I think my disguise is fairly ruined."

Smiling, he tossed the muslin onto the table. "You can leave through the back so no one sees you, and I'll fetch a hack. First, I'll inform 'Mr. Gates' that you became ill."

Isabelle giggled as she drew her shirt over her head. Val pulled her breeches up over her legs and gently lifted her down from the table. He started to help her tuck the shirt into the waistband, then withdrew, taking a step back.

"If I start touching you again, I won't be able to stop."

"And I wouldn't ask you to," she said huskily. She wanted him again already and feared she'd want him forever.

He tore his tortured gaze from hers and, turning from her, found his own shirt. Pulling the garment over his head, he cloaked her delightful view. His back was as splendid as his front, from the angles of his shoulder blades to the muscles running down to his backside. Though it was encased in breeches—a marvelously fitting pair that were nearly as snug as buckskins—she could still appreciate the fine curve of him.

When they were both dressed, Val took her hands and kissed the palm of each one.

"Shall we do this again in another ten years?" she quipped.

His winced, his forehead creasing. "Please don't make me wait that long."

What did he mean? Was he proposing they continue? That they have an affair? The temptation was great, but she'd meant what she'd told him—she couldn't become his mistress and then expect to be a headmistress at a school. But what if she was going to run a circulating library instead?

Except you can't afford a circulating library.

Resisting the urge to stamp her foot in frustration, Isabelle caressed his cheek. "We surrendered to one night. Nothing more."

Then he said the one thing she'd never imagined. And the one thing she could never say yes to. "Marry me, Isabelle."

CHAPTER 13

$\mathcal{T}$he surprise in Isabelle's eyes mirrored what Val felt. The proposal had tumbled from his mouth before he could think better of it. Could he? Think better of it?

They were clearly well matched in temperament, wit, and certainly physically. She would not be the kind of wife Louisa had been, of that he was confident.

When she failed to answer, just continued to stare at him as if he'd suggested they fly to the moon, he spoke. "You're shocked. In truth, I am shocked. Only think of it, Isabelle. We are quite good together, and we could do this every night."

"You want to marry me so that we may have intercourse whenever we like."

When she said it like that, in a halting, somewhat disbelieving manner, it sounded less than wonderful. Which was silly. "There are far worse reasons to marry."

"Yes, there are, and I've married for them." Her eyes dimmed with sadness, and he knew she was going to refuse. "I can't marry you. You know how I feel about my independence. I surrendered it once, and I won't do so again, certainly not for the convenience of bed sport."

"Why did you marry your husband?"

She let out a laugh, but it was dark and hollow. "I married him because my father recommended him, and he was of adequate means to take care of me. He was also kind and well-read, which I appreciated. But I soon learned it was all an act. He was a solitary man with a cool disposition. I'd expected a home and a family, but I got neither. When he died, he left me with enough debt to see me nearly bankrupt—so there was no home—and of course, there were no children."

He heard the ache in her voice and recalled the way she cared for Barkley's daughters, and his lungs constricted. "I am not like that."

"No, I can't imagine you are," she said softly, a smile tinged with regret lifting her lips. "But you are still offering a marriage of convenience, and I can't accept that. Besides, you need an heir, and I almost certainly can't provide you with one. You must want a child, especially after what happened with your wife."

She knew. How did she know? Viola had to have told her. What else had she revealed? The pain and fury of being a cuckold was something he'd had to learn to overcome. He hadn't been a laughingstock exactly, but he'd heard the murmurs and seen the pity. Now, having Isabelle know of it brought the anguish searing back.

"It wasn't my child." He barely recognized his own voice, so low and bitterly cold.

Her lips parted. She hadn't known that part. "Oh, Val." She stepped toward him, but he didn't want her comfort. He didn't want her to bloody *know.*

He backed away. "I think that ruined me for

wanting a child, actually. And a wife. You're quite right to refuse me." He forced his shoulders to relax, to put on a display of relief. Shouldn't he feel that way? He no more wanted to marry than she did. She was right—he wanted a convenient shag with the finest lover he'd ever had.

She deserved better than that.

"Wait here, and I'll fetch Viola and put you both in a hack." He moved the barrel out of the way and left the brewery room, closing the door behind him.

The tavern was alive with laughter and cheer, but none of it permeated his shell of self-recrimination. He never should have allowed things to progress with Isabelle. They were not careless youths. They knew better. *He* knew better.

All he'd done was reopen the wound of loss, of knowing he'd never find happiness and that he wasn't meant to.

The noise was loudest in the billiard room where Viola was in the thick of things. She'd just made a shot that had garnered a cacophony of shouts and tankards clanking together. Though her grin was cloaked with a fake beard, he would know it anywhere. Her gaze found his, and her smile dimmed.

He waited for her near the door. It took several minutes for her to extricate herself from the celebration and make her way to his side.

"Excellent timing," she said quietly. "I just won my game."

"Timing or not, you're leaving. Come on." He spun on his heel without waiting to see if she followed him.

Partway through the private salon, she snagged his sleeve and caught up to him. "What's wrong?"

"Mr. Beaufort is ill."

Viola's eyes widened. "Oh no. I had no idea she —*he*—couldn't hold his liquor."

They moved into the kitchen, and Val pulled her into the storage room. "She isn't bloody ill. Her disguise is…compromised, and you need to leave."

Viola's brow arched beneath the brim of her hat. "Compromised?"

Val scowled at her. "She was compromised the moment you brought her here. She doesn't know how to look or act like a man. She isn't like you." His gaze dipped over his sister, who'd spent the last two years perfecting her ability to pass as a gentleman.

"I thought it would be fun," she said. "Plus, I thought the two of you should spend some time together, and it looks as though I was right. You were gone for a while." Her look held a bit of a scold, as if this was somehow his fault.

"You brought her here hoping we would spend time together? What the hell are you doing meddling in my life?"

"Shhh!" She looked past him toward the kitchen. "Do you want someone to hear you?"

"Don't ignore the question."

"I wasn't meddling. I was facilitating." She huffed out a breath. "Never mind. Clearly, I made a mistake. Let's go." She pushed past him and stalked into the kitchen, then stopped short and spun back around. "Where is she?"

"Brewery."

Viola walked through the kitchen and opened the door to the brewery. Isabelle stood just inside, her disguise back in place with the exception of the beard, which she held in her hand. She looked at Viola with a weak smile. "I'm afraid I can't stick this back on."

"It isn't necessary," Val said. "You're leaving anyhow. Just keep your head down as we leave and once we get outside." He led them from the brewery into the kitchen and then out through the back entrance to the alley.

Circling around the building, they made their way out to the Haymarket, where Val promptly hailed a hack. He looked at Viola. "I'm instructing him to drive you directly home and to inform me if you request otherwise."

She rolled her eyes. "There's no need to be an autocrat."

Val opened the door but stopped himself from helping either of them inside since that would look incredibly...wrong. As the hack rumbled away, he considered going home himself.

But Barkley was at home. For one more night.

Val went back to the Wicked Duke, but didn't feel like rejoining anyone. As he made his way through the kitchen, one of the employees approached him. "Your Grace?"

He turned to her with a weary exhalation. "Yes, Mary?"

"I found this in the brewery." She handed him the length of muslin that had bound Isabelle's breasts.

"Thank you." He took the fabric, and she dipped a curtsey before returning to her work.

Val left the kitchen and started toward the office. Just before he reached the doorway, he instead opened the door to the narrow staircase that led to the rooms above. Doyle lodged there, and they kept a chamber where Val and Cole used to sleep on occasion. Back in the early days of the pub when they'd practically lived here.

He rubbed the muslin between his thumb and forefinger, imagining he could still feel the warmth of her skin. He lifted the fabric to his nose and, closing his eyes, inhaled deeply. Lilies and Isabelle, the most intoxicating scent in the world.

He discarded his coat and boots, then went to lie on one of the two cots. He glanced over at the empty one and thought of Cole, who would be married soon. Who was so deeply in love, he couldn't see straight. Whose future was so bright with promise that it was positively blinding.

Envy snaked through Val's veins. He'd never felt such optimism, such happiness, and he never would.

Folding the muslin, he held it to his chest as he lay back and closed his eyes. He might not have a future, but he had the past. And tonight, his past had become even more remarkable.

Right now he couldn't decide if that made him happy or sad.

~

*I*t was impossible to completely avoid the dowager and Viola, but over the past two days, Isabelle had done her best. When she wasn't working at the library, she was there "familiarizing" herself with the inventory. Or so she told Mr. Dangerfield. Not that he minded having her there.

Staying with the dowager had already been awkward, but after what had happened with Val on Monday night at the Wicked Duke, it was almost untenable.

Happened?

That made it sound as if it was something she hadn't been able to control. Rain happened. Spilled tea happened. Running into your one-time lover in his house while you were working as a governess happened. But rekindling that relationship, even if only for one night, wasn't something that *happened*. That was something one must choose.

And Isabelle had chosen it. Furthermore, just as with the first time, she refused to regret it. Oh, she *should*, just as she should have the first time, but contrition had never been her strong suit.

The wind was cold as she made her way across the square to the dowager's house. A footman opened the door, and she hurried inside, shivering.

"Mrs. Cortland, there is a letter for you," the dowager announced from the library.

Isabelle gave her cloak, hat, and gloves to the footman and took a deep breath before going in to face Val's grandmother.

She sat in her favorite chair next to the fireplace, a cup of tea—nearly empty now—beside her on a small table. "It's over on the table there. I was going to have it delivered to your room, but hoped you'd return so you could open it with me."

Isabelle went to the table and picked up the missive. It was marked from Oxford. Her pulse sped as she opened the parchment.

It was from Mrs. Featherstone, the headmistress of one of the schools she'd written to. Mrs. Featherstone's School for the Development of Young Ladies was located in Oxford. She'd known Isabelle's parents, and if Isabelle hadn't been educated at home, she would have gone there.

Mrs. Featherstone was considering retirement and invited Isabelle to work for her with the potential to take over the school as soon as next January. It was more than Isabelle had hoped for. It was—or it had been—her dream.

Wasn't it her dream anymore?

She thought of the circulating library and how well it suited her. However, that wasn't what gave her pause. Frustration raked her from the inside out. Why was she hesitating at all? This was everything she wanted.

Only it wasn't. It seemed Val was everything she wanted.

And couldn't have.

"Is it good news?" the dowager asked, startling Isabelle from her dismal thoughts.

"It could be," Isabelle replied. "There may be a job for me in Oxford at a girls' school."

"How splendid." The dowager sipped from her teacup and set it back down. "I was going to tell you that I may know of a family in need of a governess. They're in Bath, but I didn't think you would mind that since you've never lived in London before."

"No, I wouldn't mind that." Hadn't she said distance would solve her problems? She wanted to laugh at her naïveté. Distance wouldn't solve the ache she had for Val. Time certainly hadn't.

"I could arrange for you to travel to Bath to meet them," the dowager offered.

Two possibilities now. Two *opportunities* to secure her future. Two chances to run away from Val. Not that he was pursuing her. He'd made his relief at not having to marry her quite clear.

But she didn't want to be a governess anymore. "Thank you, Your Grace, but I think I'd prefer to pursue a position other than governess."

The dowager cocked her head to the side, and her gaze softened. It was the kindest expression Isabelle had ever seen her wear. "Because of Lord Barkley, I presume. I wish I could tell you that would never happen again, but the plight of governesses is well known."

Isabelle *hadn't* been thinking of that, but she would have. "It's more than that, to be honest. I found it difficult to leave the Misses Spelman, and I would have to do it again." And again. And again.

"I see. Surely you could school yourself to maintain a bit of distance, knowing what you know now." The tone of the dowager's voice made it apparent she determined this effort would be of no consequence.

She would likely find Isabelle's preference to avoid having to do that a sign of weakness.

"Even so, I think I'd rather not be a governess again. Because of Lord Barkley." If that was the reasoning the dowager could accept, that was the reasoning Isabelle would cite.

The dowager nodded. "I understand." She started to rise, then sat back down again. "This blessed cold has made my legs so stiff."

Isabelle rushed to help her up. "Are you going upstairs?"

"Yes, I need to choose my gown for this evening. I'm taking His Grace to Almack's. *Finally.*" She said the last with a note of triumph.

Isabelle tried not to deflate in utter defeat.

"When will you know if this position at the girls' school will be forthcoming?" the dowager asked. "If you'd like to travel to Oxford, I'd be happy to arrange it. You could even leave tomorrow."

It was possible she was simply being kind, but Isabelle heard the note of anticipation in the dowager's voice. Isabelle had known staying here would be temporary, and she decided it was probably time to go.

"I would like that, thank you."

"I'll arrange it now." The dowager left, her gait more stilted than normal due to her aching joints.

Isabelle returned to the table to pick up the letter. When she turned to exit the library, she nearly ran into Viola, who breezed inside wielding her notebook, a pencil jutting from her hair.

"Grandmama said you're going to Oxford tomorrow about a teaching position. Is that true?" Viola seemed less enthusiastic than the dowager, her expression even slightly distressed.

"Yes." Isabelle held up the letter. "I received an invitation from one of the schools I wrote to."

"That's...wonderf—" Viola pressed her lips together. "No, it's terrible."

Isabelle blinked at her. "It is?"

"Well, yes! I, er, I need you." Viola put her hand on her hip. "I've never had a chaperone I liked before."

Isabelle was skeptical. "Have you ever even had a chaperone?"

"No. But that doesn't disprove my statement."

Isabelle couldn't resist the smile that rose to her lips. "While I appreciate that very much, I am not a chaperone. I don't accompany you to any events, nor would I want to. I wouldn't know how to behave at a rout or, heaven forbid, a ball."

"Why wouldn't you?" Viola seemed genuinely interested.

"I don't dance, for one."

"As my chaperone, you wouldn't need to dance. Anyway, I rarely dance either." She lifted her hand from her hip and slashed it through the air. "Only when Val or one of his friends asks me because they're trying to avoid dancing with anyone else. If you came with me, you'd be my ally on the perimeter, my confidante. Well, along with my friends."

Isabelle could imagine those friends were likely sisters or daughters of dukes themselves. She would be utterly outclassed. "If you're trying to persuade me, you're failing, I'm afraid. And please don't think I don't appreciate your kindness, but I am far more fond of books and learning than parties and socializing."

"Oh, I'm not being kind," Viola said. "I'm being selfish. You would love my friends. They are also fond of books and learning. You and Felicity would get along exceedingly well, I think. And now that Diana's joined us, I am confident you and she would be thick as thieves."

"Are you playing matchmaker?"

Viola's head snapped up, her sky-blue eyes wide. "Absolutely not." Her reaction was both rapid and intense.

"With friends, I mean," Isabelle clarified, though now another thought was taking root...

"Oh, well then, yes. I haven't even begun to tell you about Priscilla. You may like her best of all."

Isabelle considered Viola's behavior—today as well as Monday when they'd left the Wicked Duke. In the hack, she'd asked if Isabelle was truly ill. Preferring to avoid conversation entirely, particularly anything to do with Val, she'd said yes. Even so, Viola had asked if Val had taken care of her since they'd been gone together for so long. Isabelle had responded with a vague "Somewhat." Then she'd laid her head against the side of the hack and closed her eyes, effectively putting an end to further interrogation.

In hindsight, Isabelle had to wonder if Viola had organized the entire thing—well, obviously not the *entire* thing. She was aware that Isabelle and Val had some sort of closer association than they'd acknowledged. Both she and Val had been foolish enough in their actions and words.

"Viola, are you playing *actual* matchmaker?"

Feigned surprise was quickly followed by resignation and then total accountability. "Yes. Someone has to. You and Val are apparently never going to find your way to each other on your own."

They had too. Twice. At least temporarily. "There is no future for Val and me. He is a duke. I am—at present anyway—a librarian."

Viola waved a hand. "Bah. Do you love him?"

Did she love him? It wasn't a question, at least not in her mind. Of course she loved him. She'd loved him as a naïve girl ten years ago, she'd loved him when she'd had nothing else to love, and she loved him now—not because of who he'd been or who she remembered, but because of who he was today. A man who cared for others and encouraged them to be who they were meant to be. When he'd told her about why he and Colehaven had founded the Wicked Duke, she'd been moved by their egalitarian ideals, which they'd possessed at Oxford and had clearly maintained even as they'd donned and worn the mantle of duke.

But her love for him didn't matter. He didn't love her, and he was a duke. Most of Society didn't share his ideals, and they'd eat her—a librarian and the daughter of a teacher and the granddaughter of a country vicar—alive.

Viola exhaled. "Never mind. I can see that you do, even if you cannot. This must have been a whirlwind romance. You just met, what, a fortnight ago?"

For some reason, the truth spilled from Isabelle's mouth. What did it matter to keep it secret from Viola? "We met at Oxford."

"You're joking." Viola gaped at her, then realization dawned, and she nodded slowly. "Of course you aren't. Continue. Please."

"Val—His Grace—and I kept running into each other in town."

"Knowing my brother, there was nothing of chance about those encounters," Viola said wryly.

Isabelle smiled. "No, there was not. He was rather persistent. Anyway, that is how and when we met."

Viola moved to the table, where she deposited her notebook and perched on the edge, a stance that would horrify her grandmother. "Why didn't he just marry you then?"

"Because he didn't want to?" Isabelle let out a nervous laugh. They'd never discussed marriage—at least not to each other. She'd told him that her father had a suitor in mind for her, and that man had eventually become her husband. Val had told her that his grandmother had a list of young ladies he should consider courting, even though he'd made it clear he didn't wish to wed for several more years. None of those things had given her any encouragement that he might wed her, and why should they have?

"I don't think that's true. I think he's just a block-head," Viola said, crossing her arms over her chest.

"It doesn't matter since we can't marry. As I said before, he's a duke and I'm a librarian."

"And I told you that doesn't matter. Or if I didn't explicitly, I meant to. Let me say it now: there's no magic to being a duchess. You're clever, graceful, and my grandmother likes you. You're already leagues ahead of most duchesses."

"But I don't want to be a duchess." There, she'd said it. She was terrified of being at the center of Society's interest and gossip.

"Even with Val at your side?" Viola's voice was so full of hope, her gaze so awash with anticipation, that Isabelle could almost be swept up in her enthusiasm. Almost.

"Not even with Val at my side." An ache rooted in Isabelle's chest and began to spread. "I need to go pack for my trip."

"You're still going?"

"Of course. Nothing has changed now that you know the truth, Viola." *Some* of the truth. The real truth would remain buried deep inside Isabelle, where she could keep it safe and treasure it in the days to come. "I am still in need of a job, and your grandmother has been kind enough to help me in my time of need. She's already arranged for my journey, and I won't disrespect her by changing my mind."

Viola made an inelegant sound with her lips. "All right. But I will say, I don't think my grandmother would feel disrespected if she knew you and Val loved each other. She'd want you to marry. She's *desperate* for him to remarry."

So desperate that even Isabelle would do? She wasn't sure how she felt about that, and thankfully, it didn't matter since it would never come to pass.

Isabelle summoned a smile for Viola, sorry that their friendship was over just as it had barely begun. "Thank you for your support."

"You shall always have it." Her tone and gaze were both warm and determined.

Isabelle turned and left before the ache in her chest swallowed her whole.

CHAPTER 14

*V*iola swept Val with an assessing appraisal from head to toe. "Don't you look splendid."

Val blinked at his sister standing in the center of his entrance hall. He took in her heavy cloak and the boots peeking out from beneath the hem. She was not dressed for Almack's, but then she never went to Almack's. "Why is it Grandmama never forces you to go to Almack's as she does me?"

"Because I am not husband shopping."

He strode farther into the entrance hall. "And why not? Why are you excused from the Marriage Mart while I am not? I actually tried the bloody estate of marriage, unlike you."

"You know why I didn't marry," she said quietly.

Yes, he did. "Why are you here?"

"I came to tell you that Isabelle is leaving in the morning for Oxford. She has an opportunity at a school there."

Val's muscles bunched as his heart began to pound. He worked to keep his equilibrium. "Good for her."

"That's it? That's all you have to say?" Viola

groaned and rolled her eyes. "You are the most idiot-ic…" she muttered.

"What am I supposed to say?"

Viola threw her hands up. "Oh, I don't know. That you love her? That you can't live without her? But maybe I've read this entire situation wrong. First, she won't admit she loves you and insists she can't be a duchess, and now you're behaving as if she's just another person instead of the woman who stole your heart ten years ago."

Val gaped at her. "The what?"

"She told me all about Oxford. Maybe not *all* about it, but I'm not stupid like *some* people." She looked at him from the side of her eye. "So are you going to pretend you don't love her either?"

Pretend. Yes, that's precisely what he'd done for a decade now. He'd pretended their night together was something he could keep locked away, that the love he'd felt for her could be ignored. The love he still felt for her.

"No."

Viola stared at him, her eyes widening to an im-possible diameter and her jaw dropping. "You aren't going to argue with me?"

"Apparently not."

She snapped her mouth closed and finally blinked. "I honestly don't know how to react. I may need a vinaigrette."

"I would douse you in the contents if you'd just be quiet." He said that because she expected him to. Right now, he actually wanted to kiss her with grati-tude. "She doesn't want to be a duchess?"

"Do you want to make her one?"

"I think I do." He'd already asked her at the Wicked Duke, but that had been a reaction he hadn't entirely thought through. Now he had. He wanted to marry her.

His insides somersaulted. He'd cocked it up so badly the last time. It wasn't that he'd chosen Louisa. None of it had been her fault.

"You think?" Viola stepped toward him, her forehead creasing. "I know you're afraid, but Isabelle isn't Louisa."

"Louisa deserved far better," he said softly, keeping his voice low. "All she ever wanted was for me to love her. I tried, truly I did. But my heart already belonged to someone else."

"Isabelle."

He nodded. "Louisa did what anyone would in the face of rejection."

"I would argue that not everyone would do what she did, but that doesn't matter anymore. Louisa is gone, and you can't change the past. You can, however, control the present." She brushed a speck of something off his lapel. "Grandmama has taken Isabelle to Almack's."

"What?" The word exploded from Val.

Viola giggled, her eyes alight with mirth. "Shocking, isn't it? Once I explained to Grandmama that you would find your duchess *tonight* if she only took Isabelle with her, she completely understood. She had to work quickly to obtain a voucher, but you know how the patronesses adore her. If the patronesses had a patroness, it would be Grandmama."

A truer statement had never been made.

"Honestly, the hardest part was convincing Isabelle to go. Indeed, I fear she may change her mind. I had to leave to come here before they departed."

Val could imagine Isabelle not wanting to go to Almack's, particularly since he never wanted to go. Until now. Suddenly, Almack's was the only place he wanted to be—so long as she was there. "Do you think she went?"

Viola shrugged. "There is only one way to find

out. You go, and I'll go home. If she's not at Almack's, you'll know where to come."

He leaned down and kissed his sister's cheek. "Thank you. I shall owe you for this."

"Yes, but pray do not repay me in kind." She shuddered with revulsion. "I do not want you matchmaking for me."

"Life may surprise you, sister." He winked at her, then went toward the door where the footman met him with his gloves and hat.

He dashed to his waiting coach and instructed the coachman to make the best possible time. He'd never been so eager to get to Almack's in his life.

~

*A*s Isabelle walked into the hallowed ballroom at Almack's, she wondered how on earth she'd allowed the dowager duchess to persuade her to come. The answer, of course, was simple: she was the Dowager Duchess of Eastleigh, and one did not refuse the Dowager Duchess of Eastleigh.

But now that Isabelle was here beneath the glittering chandeliers and amidst the ton's most elite, Isabelle was beginning to regret her decision. She glanced over at the dowager, whose expression could only be described as pleasant hauteur. The ostrich feathers atop her head gave her additional height, making her seem an even bigger presence than she already was. Though they'd just arrived, everyone around them was looking in her direction and murmuring as they cast looks—some surreptitious and others openly curious—in Isabelle's direction.

Self-consciously, she smoothed the side of her hair, which had been swept into an impossibly complicated style with pearls and a bandeau that sported its own violet ostrich feather. Then she brushed her gloved hand along her hip, smoothing the line of her Saxon-blue gown. It belonged to Viola, but she'd never worn it, and the dowager's maid had worked a miracle to alter it to fit Isabelle, including the addition of a violet flounce at the hem since Isabelle was a few inches taller than Viola.

Finding slippers had proven the biggest challenge and had required several footmen visiting countless cobblers and returning with a variety of footwear, all of which had been rejected by the dowager save the pair now adorning Isabelle's feet. And pinching her toes, for they were just a bit too snug.

"Come and meet the patronesses, dear." The dowager led Isabelle along the side of the ballroom to the opposite end, where several women seemed to be holding court from a group of sofas atop a dais.

Isabelle dipped into the curtsey she'd practiced too many times with Viola. The least she could have done was come with them, but she didn't have a voucher, and she'd refused to allow her grandmother to obtain one. There was a deeper reason Viola avoided certain aspects of Society, but while Viola was content to meddle in other's affairs, she did not reveal her own secrets.

And against her better judgment, Isabelle had allowed her to meddle.

After retreating to her chamber following her conversation with Viola that afternoon, Viola and the dowager had come to see her. The dowager had laid it out very clearly: if she wanted Val, she had to demonstrate that she could be a duchess, and that meant going to Almack's and holding her own amongst Society's most exclusive members.

That, of course, had done absolutely nothing to persuade Isabelle, which was why the dowager had then simply told her she was going. When Isabelle had asked why, she'd responded, "Because if my grandson is in love with you, as my granddaughter insists, then you shall give him the opportunity to recognize what a fool he is for not making you his duchess sooner."

With logic like that, how could Isabelle have refused?

After paying their respects to the patronesses, they moved to a nearby sofa along one of the longer walls. "I am going to sit," the dowager said.

"Should I also sit?" Isabelle hoped so. She felt rather vulnerable standing there. She realized she'd likely feel just as vulnerable if she hid herself in the corner all evening.

"Not until after you dance, and while the patronesses gave you permission to waltz, I'd be careful with whom you do."

Isabelle's heart began to pound, and her neck grew damp. She'd reviewed the basics of dancing with Viola in between dress fittings, but now that she was here with the orchestra playing and the dancers moving in beautiful harmony across the ballroom, she felt as if she might cast up her accounts. She'd been to an assembly or two, but that had been years ago, and it hadn't been Almack's.

Suddenly, the noise of the room diminished, the dancers became a blur, her pulse slowed. He was coming toward her. Dressed in a crisp black coat with a rich green waistcoat and the whitest, most intricately knotted cravat she'd ever seen. He was an apparition, a dream conjured by her twenty-year-old mind.

Did dreams bow?

Of course they did.

He presented his leg, then straightened to his full height. This seemed to restart everything around her—the sounds, the sights—as well as her feeling of disquiet. Her heart increased its pace once more, the cacophony of it echoing in her own ear.

Val turned to the dowager and inclined his head. "Good evening, Grandmama."

She looked up at him approvingly. "Good evening, Eastleigh."

He returned his attention to Isabelle. Her entire being thrilled at the sight of him. She didn't have to look around to see if anyone saw what she saw—everyone did. They openly gaped at him, and all she could think was that it had to be incredibly uncomfortable. And yet he seemed hardly to notice. Indeed, he seemed to notice only one thing: her.

"I would be honored if you would dance the next set with me," he said. "Will you?"

She wanted to caution him that his feet might not survive, but she could only manage a tiny squeak of a word. "Yes."

He offered his arm, and she curled her hand around his sleeve. Though she'd touched him many times, and in far more intimate ways than she currently did, this was somehow different. They were on display for all the world to see. They'd come out of the shadows and into a dazzling light. There was no going back now.

She looked up at him, and his answering gaze told her that he knew it too.

"We'll just promenade for a few moments while this set finishes," he said. "May I say you look beautiful?"

"Thank you. So do you. Handsome, rather." For a supposedly educated woman, she was having an incredibly difficult time finding words tonight.

"Thank you. I understand you are going to Oxford tomorrow."

They were going to discuss that here? Isabelle glanced about. It wasn't as if anyone could hear them over the music and conversation, even if they were staring.

"Yes. Mrs. Featherstone invited me. She is considering retirement. It's possible a year from now I could be headmistress of my own school." She looked at him sideways, waiting for his reaction.

"That's precisely what you wanted." He didn't sound nearly as enthusiastic as he should, but then, she didn't feel nearly as enthusiastic as *she* should.

"Yes."

The music finished, and he stopped, turning toward her. "Are you ready to dance?"

"No, but I will try. Have a care for your feet."

His lips spread in a grin that made her heart flip over. "Do your worst."

He led her onto the dance floor. "It's a waltz. Do you know the steps?"

"Barely." Viola had given her a cursory overview, but Isabelle had never seen it, let alone danced it.

"While you will likely have more occasion to destroy my feet in a waltz, I will also be able to guide you more carefully than in a country dance. Ready?" He gently clasped either side of her waist while she placed her hands on his shoulders. It was an alarmingly intimate dance meant to be tempered by holding each other at arm's length. However, Isabelle was far too keenly aware of his touch and where it could lead were they not in the middle of the most popular Society location in London.

Why oh why had she agreed to this?

Then the music started, and he swept her in elegant circles. The light sparkled around her, and the music hummed through her body. She was suddenly very glad she'd come.

She immersed herself in the gaiety and splendor surrounding them, laughing as she stepped on his foot for the third time. He grinned in response, seeming to be having as wonderful a time as she was. Then she began to feel a bit dizzy and, laughing, asked if they could slow down.

"I will go at whatever speed you decree." He moved her out of the way of other spinning couples so they could twirl at a more sedate pace. When the music came to a close, she found she couldn't stop smiling.

"You enjoyed that," he said, his green eyes twinkling beneath the chandeliers.

"More than I ever imagined." Whatever happened, she had no regrets. Tonight, she'd danced in the arms of the only man she'd ever loved, and nothing in the rest of her days would compare.

He offered his arm once more, and she took it, sorry that the dance was over. "I am going to leave now, but I will call on you tomorrow."

Reality tore the veil of her dream. "I'm going to Oxford tomorrow."

He looked down at her as they made their way toward the dowager. "Are you still?" He sounded a bit…surprised?

She hadn't thought about not going. Did this mean—? She had no idea what it meant, nor could she ask him to explain in the middle of Almack's when they were a dozen steps from his grandmother.

"I think so," she said, feeling utterly confused. What was happening here?

They'd arrived at the dowager's sofa. He took her hand and kissed the back. "I'll call on you tomorrow. Early."

He said good night to his grandmother and left, cutting a swath through the people who gawked as he strode by.

"Now you may sit," the dowager said, indicating the space next to her. Another woman sat at the other end of the sofa, but she was speaking with someone seated on the adjacent sofa.

Isabelle slowly sank down beside the dowager and allowed the dream to envelop her once more as she lost sight of Val's departing back.

The dowager leaned toward her. "I know you don't understand Society, so allow me to explain what has happened. The Duke of Eastleigh is an unmarried man in want of a wife. He came to Almack's, *the* definitive Marriage Mart in London, a destination he never frequents, and danced the waltz with precisely one woman: *you*. Then he left. He spoke to no one, and barely reserved more than a handful of words for me."

Isabelle's pulse couldn't seem to regain a normal pace at all since she'd arrived. "I see." She didn't really, but also didn't want to aggravate the dowager.

"You will not be asked to dance again because it seems clear Eastleigh has singled you out, and because you are sitting with me. I frighten some people —those people are generally fools. People, and not just the fools, are now wondering if you will become the next Duchess of Eastleigh. Idiotic wagers may even be taking place."

One visit to Almack's and one dance, and she was precisely where she'd never wanted to be: at the heart of Society's gossip. She shifted uncomfortably. "You're saying the expectation is for me to marry him. But he hasn't even asked me." Only he had, and she'd refused him. And he was going to call on her tomorrow.

Oh, she was terribly stupid. He was going to propose again. Furthermore, he'd conveyed his intentions rather clearly to anyone with a thimbleful more of knowledge and experience than Isabelle. Which was the entire ballroom of nearly a thousand people.

Isabelle was in the corner once more. The

freedom she so dearly treasured was at risk. And this time, she found she…didn't care. What's more, she didn't particularly want to be independent if it meant she wasn't with Val.

She peered at the dowager in suspicion, thinking she and Viola were perhaps two of the most calculating people she'd ever encountered. "Did you bring me here so that I would feel as though I couldn't refuse him?"

The dowager's eyes sparked with anger. "Do you love my grandson?" She spoke quietly, but the urgency in her tone was unmistakable. "Do not prevaricate with me."

Giddiness bubbled in Isabelle's chest, and she tried very hard not to smile at the dowager, who would surely find it vulgar. "Yes."

"Then none of this matters. Tomorrow, he will propose, you will accept, and that is that." She took a deep breath and resettled her features into a mask of serenity. "Now, enjoy yourself, dear. Have a glass of punch, though it's disappointingly bland. One would think they would correct that."

They stayed another two hours, during which many people came to be introduced to Isabelle. Their curiosity was obvious, as was an underlying current of envy from some of the women, particularly a few mothers whose primary objective was marrying off their daughter or daughters. Or so the dowager had explained. It was a dizzying evening, and not because of the waltz. Isabelle couldn't hope to remember all the names or anecdotes or silly rules she'd learned. And yet, she would try.

After all, her future depended on it.

CHAPTER 15

*A*fter trying to distract himself at the Wicked Duke, first with ale, then with billiards, then with cards in the private salon, Val abandoned the evening and went home. The town house was quiet now that Barkley and his family were gone, but for the first time, it felt…lonely.

He'd left the tavern because it now reminded him of Isabelle at every turn. And now, apparently, he couldn't even relax at home because she haunted him here.

She will be with you always, you dolt.

He'd stripped down to his shirtsleeves and picked up the length of muslin, which he'd tucked under his pillow the past two nights like some sort of lovesick lad. Closing his eyes, he inhaled Isabelle's scent, praying that very soon, she'd be with him in the flesh.

What if she refused him again? It was one thing to acknowledge that he loved her desperately, that he always had, but what if she didn't love him in return?

How will you know until you tell her so, you dolt?

Val opened his eyes and scowled. "Stop that."

"Who are you talking to, Your Grace?" His valet,

Ross, had quietly entered the chamber and picked up his discarded coat and waistcoat.

"No one."

Inclining his head, Ross asked if he'd like anything before bed.

"No, thank you, Ross."

A knock on his chamber door drew them both to turn their heads. Ross went and answered the summons, then turned toward Val. "You've a visitor."

"At this hour?"

"Apparently so," Ross said evenly. "A...lady."

Val was at the door in a trice, opening it wide to reveal his butler. "Who is it, Sadler?"

"Mrs. Cortland, Your Grace."

Pushing past both retainers, Val started toward the stairs. Had something happened? Ice shot through his veins.

"She's in the library," Sadler called after him.

Val bounded down the stairs, his stockinged feet skidding across the marble at the base as he vaulted toward the library. The door was open, and as he raced across the threshold, she pivoted from the hearth where she stood warming her hands in front of the fire.

"It's rather cold tonight," she said.

He rushed forward, scanning her for injury. "Are you all right?"

She looked up at him, her eyes alight with... something. "Perfect."

"You shouldn't be here. This is highly—"

"Scandalous, yes. But if my suspicions are correct, it won't matter." She shrugged. "Even if they aren't, it doesn't matter." She straightened and looked him in the eye. "I came to tell you that I love you."

Joy unfurled in his chest, but it was checked by a sliver of...disappointment? "I wanted to say it first."

Her eyes widened briefly, and she covered her mouth to stifle a short laugh. "I beg your pardon?"

"I love you, Isabelle. I always have, even when I should have let you go." He winced, then turned his attention from her, gazing into the flames in the grate while he pushed his hand through his hair.

She touched his sleeve. "What do you mean?"

He took her hand and brought it to his mouth, kissing the back, her palm, her wrist. Then he looked at her once more. "I was a terrible husband to my first wife. Viola told you what she was like, but I think she was just trying to gain my attention. All she wanted was for me to love her, and I couldn't."

She cupped the side of his face. "My darling, I am sure you tried. I tried to love my husband too, and he didn't particularly care. You've no way to know how things might have been. We can only accept the way things were and are. Please accept that I love you more than anything."

Her words made his soul take flight. "More than your independence?"

"I feel confident you will allow me a measure of independence most duchesses do not enjoy."

"You know me very well. What of your occupation? You love teaching."

"Actually, I find I love being a librarian even more. Would it be scandalous if I started a circulating library?"

"I can't say that I care." He began to remove the pins holding her bandeau in place. "Besides, you've established a level of scandal by coming here tonight that a circulating library cannot remotely touch."

She laughed again, a low, gorgeous sound that filled him with love and hope and joy. And desire.

He froze. "Does my grandmother know you're here?"

"No, but Viola does. She's covering for me. Your sister is a devious strategist."

"Thankfully, in this case, she's used her power for good." He wrapped his arms around her waist and pulled her against him. "To answer your question from earlier, if, in fact, it was a question, my proposal of marriage still stands, though the idea of making you my mistress holds a wicked appeal."

She twined her arms around his neck. "Does it? Well then, perhaps I should be your mistress—at least for one night."

He laughed softly. "Seems like we've done that before."

"Not formally."

"No, not formally. We've never done anything formally." And he wanted to. She deserved that and so much more. He dropped to his knees in front of her, his hands on her waist. "Isabelle, will you do me the very great honor of becoming my duchess?"

"Before I say yes, and I desperately want to say yes, what of my inability to have children?"

"To that I say, time will tell. If we are not blessed with a child, I will never regret marrying you. Can you say the same?" He held his breath awaiting her answer, and thankfully, she was quick.

"Yes. To both questions." She touched his cheek. "How did I get so lucky?" she whispered.

He saw the tears in her eyes and hoped they were from happiness. "I know you never wanted this, but I promise I will make all your dreams come true."

She nodded, smiling broadly, and he knew she was as happy as he was. "You already have. Now stand up and kiss me."

He did.

EPILOGUE

"*T*his is hardly fair," Colehaven complained as champagne was distributed around the drawing room. "You just had to marry before me. *Again*."

Val laughed in response, and Isabelle stared up at him, not quite believing that as of twenty minutes ago, she was the Duchess of Eastleigh.

"I suppose I will make a toast," Colehaven announced. "To my dear friend and his lovely wife, whom he will need to work *very* hard to deserve." He looked between Val and Isabelle, his eyes full of love and joy. "I am so glad you've found each other *at last*." He raised his glass, and everyone did the same.

Everyone being the dowager, Viola, Colehaven's delightful fiancée, Diana, whom Isabelle already adored as Viola said she would, Hugh Tarleton, who'd performed the ceremony, and, most importantly to Isabelle, Beatrice and Caroline. Lord and Lady Barkley were also in attendance, but they stood somewhat in the background, because they were either aware of their unpopularity in this company or Val had instructed them to do so. She wouldn't have put it past him to do that.

Last night, he'd told her in satisfying detail of

how he'd asked Barkley to leave and threatened him in rather direct terms. He'd instructed Miss Shipley to notify him if Barkley even *hinted* of overstepping and pledged to do the same with any other governess they might hire.

They'd discussed many things last night—their marriages, their stupidity, and their pledge to never waste another moment. That had been in between rediscovering each other's bodies. Then they'd risen very early. Val had dropped Isabelle in Berkeley Square on his way to Doctors' Commons to procure the special license. Following had been a whirlwind of activity to prepare for the wedding this afternoon, which the dowager had grudgingly approved of.

"It is not what I would have chosen," she'd said, "but I shall count my blessings that Eastleigh is marrying again, and this time, he chose wisely."

Nothing she'd said could have made Isabelle feel any more welcome. Viola was a bit more effusive in her excitement, saying how thrilled she was to finally have a sister and promising more adventures like the one at the Wicked Duke. Isabelle hadn't wanted to tell her that she had all the adventure she needed with becoming a duchess.

She was still uncertain how she would fare, but with Val by her side and the support of the dowager, she knew she would manage. Things had turned out far better than she could ever have dreamed. She only wished her father were here to see it.

Later, when everyone had left and it was just her and Val snuggled on the settee before the fire in the drawing room, Isabelle could no longer hide her exhaustion. In fact, they both yawned at the same time, causing a fit of laughter.

"We should retire," Val suggested.

"Before dinner?" Isabelle lifted her head from his shoulder. "Won't the staff find that strange?"

"They'd better get used to it. I foresee many evenings where we retire early." He waggled his brows at her, and she laughed again.

"I'm not sure I can keep my eyes open." She yawned once more, lifting her hand to cover her mouth.

He readjusted himself and leaned down to nuzzle her neck before trailing his lips along her jaw. "Your eyes don't need to be open."

Threading her fingers through his hair, she brought his head up so she could kiss him. Their lips met with a passion that belied their exhaustion. After several long moments, she pulled back. "I surrender."

He exhaled. "I'm afraid you can't. I already surrendered to you long ago. Before I even knew it myself."

"We belong to each other, then." She looked at him with wicked promise.

He stood from the settee and swept her into his arms with a smile. "Always."

THE END

What happens when a stolen kiss risks a spitfire's one chance at independence? Find out in ONE NIGHT OF PASSION.

THANK YOU!

Thank you so much for reading One Night of Surrender. I hope you enjoyed it! Want to find out what happens when a stolen kiss risks a spitfire's one chance at independence? Find out in the Wicked Dukes Club, ONE NIGHT OF PASSION.

Would you like to know when my next book is available? Sign up for my reader club at http://www.darcyburke.com/readerclub, follow me on social media:

Facebook: http://facebook.com/DarcyBurkeFans
Twitter at @darcyburke
Instagram at darcyburkeauthor
Pinterest at darcyburkewrite

I hope you'll consider leaving a review at your favorite online vendor or networking site!

Follow me on Bookbub to receive updates on preorders, new releases, and deals!

Catch up with my other historical series: The Untouchables, Secrets and Scandals, and Legendary Rogues. If you like contemporary romance, I hope you'll check out my Ribbon Ridge series available from Avon Impulse, and the continuation of Ribbon Ridge in So Hot.

I appreciate my readers so much. Thank you, thank you, *thank you*.

BOOKS BY DARCY BURKE

Historical Romance

Wicked Dukes Club

One Night for Seduction by Erica Ridley
One Night of Surrender *by Darcy Burke*
One Night of Passion by Erica Ridley
One Night of Scandal by Darcy Burke
One Night to Remember by Erica Ridley
One Night of Temptation by Darcy Burke

The Spitfire Society

Never Have I Ever With a Duke
A Duke is Never Enough
A Duke Will Never Do

The Untouchables

The Forbidden Duke
The Duke of Daring
The Duke of Deception
The Duke of Desire
The Duke of Defiance
The Duke of Danger
The Duke of Ice
The Duke of Ruin
The Duke of Lies

The Duke of Seduction
The Duke of Kisses
The Duke of Distraction

Secrets and Scandals

Her Wicked Ways
His Wicked Heart
To Seduce a Scoundrel
To Love a Thief (a novella)
Never Love a Scoundrel
Scoundrel Ever After

Legendary Rogues

Lady of Desire
Romancing the Earl
Lord of Fortune
Captivating the Scoundrel

Contemporary Romance

Ribbon Ridge

Where the Heart Is (a prequel novella)
Only in My Dreams
Yours to Hold
When Love Happens
The Idea of You
When We Kiss
You're Still the One

Ribbon Ridge: So Hot

So Good
So Right
So Wrong

ABOUT THE AUTHOR

Darcy Burke is the USA Today Bestselling Author of sexy, emotional historical and contemporary romance. Darcy wrote her first book at age 11, a happily ever after about a swan addicted to magic and the female swan who loved him, with exceedingly poor illustrations. Join her Reader Club at http://www.darcyburke.com/readerclub.

A native Oregonian, Darcy lives on the edge of wine country with her guitar-strumming husband, their two hilarious kids who seem to have inherited the writing gene. They're a crazy cat family with two Bengal cats, a small, fame-seeking cat named after a fruit, and an older rescue Maine Coon who is the master of chill and five a.m. serenading. Her happy places are Disneyland and Labor Day weekend at the Gorge. Visit Darcy online at http://www.darcyburke.com and follow her social media: Facebook at http://www.facebook.com/darcyburkefans, Twitter @darcyburke at http://www.twitter.com/darcyburke, Instagram at http://www.instagram/darcyburkeauthor, and Pinterest at http://www.pinterest.com/darcyburkewrite.